Jake laughed shortly. "I'm not even in a relationship. How am I supposed to find someone to marry me?"

Calista looked from the baby to him and, without hesitation, said, "You could ask me."

Jake stared at her, stunned. The woman his daughter took to so readily couldn't possibly have meant what he thought she'd just said.

"Ask you what?" he asked her, enunciating each word slowly.

"Ask me to marry you. Because I would."

Dear Reader,

This is my first visit to Thunder Canyon, Montana. (Love that name. Can't you just see the cowboys heading them off at the pass?) A town, I've been told, that has been around for a while.

This is the place that Jake Castro turns to when the world as he knows it crumbles on him. A New Orleans cop who suddenly finds himself a single dad to an infant when his former partner, Maggie O'Shea, is killed in the line of duty, he comes to Thunder Canyon and his family for the emotional support—and help with diapers—he needs. The latter is supplied, along with humor and understanding, by Calista Clifton, his sister Erin's friend. A recent college graduate, Calista has her eye on a career in politics and to that end is already an intern working in the mayor's office. Coming from a family of eight, Calista is an old hand at knowing exactly what babies need. She also, as the story progresses, intuitively knows just what emotionally shell-shocked Jake needs. A little TLC. Neither one of them expected to find love at this point in their lives, but that was the bonus that life in Thunder Canyon provided.

As always, I thank you for taking the time to read my book and from the bottom of my heart, I wish you someone to love who loves you back.

Love,

Marie Ferrarella

THE BABY WORE A BADGE

MARIE FERRARELLA

Harlequin

SPECIAL EDITION

Special thanks and acknowledgment to Marie Ferrarella for
her contribution to the Montana Mavericks continuity.

ISBN-13: 978-0-373-65613-4

THE BABY WORE A BADGE

Recycling programs
for this product may
not exist in your area.

Selected Books by Marie Ferrarella

Harlequin Special Edition

°*Fortune's Just Desserts* #2107
¶*A Match for the Doctor* #2117
¶*What the Single Dad Wants* #2122
‡*The Baby Wore a Badge* #2131

Silhouette Special Edition

~*Diamond in the Rough* #1910
~*The Bride with No Name* #1917
~*Mistletoe and Miracles* #1941
††*Plain Jane and the Playboy* #1946
~*Travis's Appeal* #1958
Loving the Right Brother #1977
The 39-Year-Old Virgin #1983
~*A Lawman for Christmas* #2006
¤¤*Prescription for Romance* #2017
¶*Doctoring the Single Dad* #2031
¶*Fixed Up with Mr. Right?* #2041
¶*Finding Happily-Ever-After* #2060
¶*Unwrapping the Playboy* #2084

°°Forever, Texas
*Cavanaugh Justice
†The Doctors Pulaski
~Kate's Boys
††The Fortunes of Texas:
   Return to Red Rock
¤¤The Baby Chase
¶Matchmaking Mamas
°The Fortunes of Texas: Lost…and Found
‡Montana Mavericks: The Texans are Coming!

Silhouette Romantic Suspense

†*A Doctor's Secret* #1503
†*Secret Agent Affair* #1511
Protecting His Witness #1515
Colton's Secret Service #1528
The Heiress's 2-Week Affair #1556
Cavanaugh Pride #1571
Becoming a Cavanaugh #1575
The Agent's Secret Baby #1580
The Cavanaugh Code #1587
In Bed with the Badge #1596
Cavanaugh Judgment #1612
Colton by Marriage #1616
Cavanaugh Reunion #1623
†*In His Protective Custody* #1644

Harlequin Romantic Suspense

Private Justice #1664

American Romance

Pocketful of Rainbows #145
°°*The Sheriff's Christmas
   Surprise* #1329
°°*Ramona and the
   Renegade* #1338
°°*The Doctor's Forever
   Family* #1346

MARIE FERRARELLA

This *USA TODAY* bestselling and RITA® Award–winning author has written more than two hundred books for Harlequin Books and Silhouette Books, some under the name Marie Nicole. Her romances are beloved by fans worldwide. Visit her website at www.marieferrarella.com.

To
Marcia Book Adirim
without whose fertile
imagination
I wouldn't have been able to write
this book.
Thank you.

Chapter One

He was burning the candle at both ends.

More than that, both ends were closing in on him. Fast.

New Orleans police officer Jake Castro dragged his hand through his unruly light blond hair as if that could somehow help him drag his mind into some sort of optimal focus instead of the dazed fog it had been in for the last few weeks, ever since his life had taken this dramatic turn that had completely changed his life.

With a deep sigh that came from the bottom of his toes, he glanced at the clock on his nightstand.

Five minutes.

That was all he'd had. Five minutes.

Five minutes of sleep before Marlie had begun to cry loud enough to wake the dead. Or, at the very least, him.

Getting up, still more than half-asleep, he stumbled over to the newly placed crib at the other end of his heretofore bachelor bedroom. Bleary-eyed, he stared down at the small occupant.

"I'll buy you a car if you let me sleep just twenty-five more minutes." His efforts at bargaining fell on completely unreceptive ears. If anything, Marlie cried even louder.

So much for bribery.

With another, now-resigned sigh, Jake reached into the crib and picked up his seven-month-old daughter.

For the moment, Marlie began to quiet down. Ordinarily, he might take some pride in that, that the baby was bonding with him, but he was way too worn out to take comfort in even that.

He was running on empty and had been for a number of days now.

"I can't keep doing this, you know," he said as he made his way over to the rocking chair, also newly acquired, as was his status as a single dad.

Marlie responded best to the swaying motion of being walked around, but Jake was far too wiped out to pace the floor. He'd pulled a long, draining shift today and had come home later than usual, a fact that had made the woman he paid to watch Marlie—Mrs. Rutherford—none too happy.

At this insane juggling act for less than three weeks and he was discovering, much to his chagrin, that he couldn't be Officer Castro, super-cop by day and then turn into super-dad at night. Somewhere in that time span he needed to get some sleep—desperately—before he had a complete meltdown.

"It's my own fault," he acknowledged, addressing his words to the tiny human being in his arms. Oblivious to her father's words, Marlie began to suck on her thumb—hard—as if it could give up some sort of sustenance if she sucked on it hard enough. "All I had to do was say 'no.' 'No, Maggie, I won't do it,' and none of this would have happened. Hell—sorry."

Jake came to a skidding halt in his self-examination. No more cursing, at least not in the house while Marlie could hear him. He'd made up the rule himself, but it wasn't easy sticking to it, especially not when he was this punchy.

"Heck," he amended, "who am I kidding? Your mother was so pigheaded she would have found someone else to say yes to her. In a heartbeat." Someone else to donate the male component that had gone into creating this tiny miracle of nature with the mighty lungs made of steel whom he was holding in his arms.

Besides, he'd been half in love with Maggie O'Shea from the first moment she had walked into the squad room and Lieutenant Franco had told him that this vision in a blue uniform was his new partner. Maggie had been sharp and witty and so damn gorgeous with all that red hair that it made him ache just to look at her.

They'd had a good relationship, both on the job and off. And they'd talked about their futures, their goals and visions. That was when he'd discovered that she was determined to be all that she could possibly be—a kick-ass police officer and a mother as well.

She'd been well on her way to becoming the first when her damn biological clock had begun to nag her. And she, in turn, had begun to subtly nag him, working on him every day, eventually relentlessly, until he had finally given in.

For a fleeting moment, he had thought they would go about it the age-old, time-honored way. But Maggie had been very up-front with him about her intentions. She'd told him that she didn't want any sort of a romantic entanglement, definitely didn't even want any sort of physical encounter happening between them.

"It's not that I don't feel attracted to you, Castro," she'd said. "It's just that I don't like complications. Never have."

Seemed ironic, in light of all the complications *he* was facing now.

She'd laid out the plan. It was all going to be very clinical, very professional. And once the process was in motion and the procedure "took," Maggie made it clear that he was free to move on. She wasn't going to ask him for anything further.

Until she'd asked him for everything.

Somewhere along the line, between agreeing to this antiseptic, clinical insemination procedure and acting as her coach in the delivery room when her actual coach couldn't be reached in time, Jake had found himself *really* falling in love with Maggie. Hard.

She'd seen it, too.

Seen it in his eyes, heard it in his voice. Enough so that it had spooked her into asking for another partner once she went back to work.

That, too, had been a bone of contention between them. She'd gone back to work a great deal sooner than he'd thought was prudent. He certainly wasn't happy about it. He didn't think she should leave Marlie so soon and secretly—or not so secretly—worried about the risks she'd be facing every day with that badge pinned to her chest.

But he couldn't talk her out of it. The more he talked, the less she heard. The upshot was that Maggie had gone back to work three months after bringing Marlie into the world.

And three months after that, she was gone.

He remembered how he'd felt when he'd heard the news over the dispatch radio. As if someone had shoved a blade right into his belly and gutted him. He remembered the speedometer reaching the other side of a hundred miles an hour as he'd raced to the hospital where they'd taken Maggie.

She'd managed to stay alive long enough for him to arrive and see her. Long enough to extract a promise from him to take care of their little girl—as if he would have allowed anyone else to take the baby. Marlie was all he had left of Maggie.

Maggie had died right after he'd said yes. Died with a smile on her lips.

Died despite the fact that he'd been holding on to her hand so tightly, trying with all his might to pull her back among the living. He must have been crazy to believe that he could.

All his efforts had naturally come to nothing. He hadn't been able to save Maggie, hadn't been able to pull her back. She'd died in front of him, leaving him to deal with monumental guilt. Guilt that had sprung from the very real belief that partner or no partner, he should have been there for Maggie, covering her back. Protecting her.

But he hadn't been able to and now Maggie was gone and he was here, trying to be what he'd been before a crack in the world had shaken his foundations, plus something new. Trying to be a father.

Right now, in his opinion, he was failing miserably at both.

Marlie began to fuss again, her displeasure growing louder. Jake recognized the cry. The infant was hungry. Did that mean he was getting better at this, or just lucky when it came to guessing?

He didn't know.

Getting up, keeping Marlie tucked against his chest, Jake made his way into the kitchen.

He already had a small saucepan half-filled with water waiting to be pressed into use on the stove. Heading straight for the refrigerator, he opened it and reached in.

Like tall, innocent soldiers, bottles of formula were standing on the top shelf. Right beside equally tall bottles of beer. They clinked slightly as he pushed a couple aside to get at the milk.

"That was your mom's favorite brand," he told Marlie, pausing to let her "look" inside. "Your mom liked to kick back at the end of the day and have one or two, just to unwind—before she was pregnant with you, of course," he qualified.

Jake closed the door with his hip, then leaned against it for a second, trying to pull himself together.

He had to stop doing this to himself, had to stop connecting every deed, every detail he came across with something to do with Maggie. Weaving her into every single second of his life was not going to change anything.

It wasn't going to bring her back.

Jake went through the familiar steps, steps he knew in his sleep now, then stood there, staring at the bottle he'd just placed into the saucepan, waiting for it to heat up.

Three minutes later, he took the bottle out, testing the liquid against the back of his wrist. It was stone-cold.

"Why isn't this—?" The rest of his question evaporated as he looked down again at the burner. No wonder the formula hadn't warmed up. He hadn't turned the burner on.

He needed help.

Putting the cold formula bottle back into the saucepan, Jake switched on the burner and turned up the temperature. Only then did he reach for the cordless phone on the wall and call his sister.

The phone rang five times on the other end. Jake

was about to hang up and redial when he heard a sleepy voice answer, whispering, "Hello?" uncertainly.

Even when she whispered, he recognized Erin's voice. "Uncle," he said, giving the universal word for surrender. "I give up. You're right. I need help. I'm in way over my head."

"Jake?" His sister still sounded somewhat confused, but she was no longer whispering hoarsely.

He heard a deep male voice in the background ask, "Who is it, Erin?"

Jake heard a noise that told him Erin was attempting to cover the receiver in a semi-bid for privacy as she apparently turned her head away to answer, "I think it's Jake."

"Yeah, it's me," Jake acknowledged. "How many other men do you know who are in over their heads?"

"No one who would call this number at two in the morning," she replied. "I thought that I was still asleep and dreaming."

"Damn—darn," Jake corrected himself again, in deference to the infant in his arms. Curbing his words was turning out to be a lot harder than he'd thought. "I forgot about the time difference," he confessed. He was calling from New Orleans. His sister lived in Thunder Canyon, Montana. "I'm sorry I woke you up. I'll call back in the morning."

"No, no," Erin insisted, her voice now clearer and insistent. "Don't hang up."

It was half a plea, half an order. Erin knew her older brother. She knew he could very well not call back in the morning. He'd sounded desperate just then. Who knew how long that would last? But while it did last, she could use it to her—and more importantly to Jake's—advantage.

Jake could be incredibly stubborn at times and making him see reason was not always an easy matter—or one that was very readily accomplished. She couldn't afford to allow this opportunity to slip right through her fingers.

"My offer to help still stands, Jake. You and the baby can stay with Corey and me for as long as you need to," she told him, referring to her brand-new husband. Like the rest of the family, he'd been there for the wedding, and then had gone back to New Orleans. "Lord knows we've got plenty of room here."

Jake laughed shortly. It wasn't that he didn't appreciate the offer—he did—it was just that he wasn't so self-centered or desperate that he couldn't put himself into his new brother-in-law's position.

"That'll sure endear me to my new brother-in-law," he told his sister. "Nothing like having a third—and part of a fourth—party around as you're trying to adjust to married life."

Erin had to concede that her brother had a point. "Okay, maybe you're right, but this isn't a small house," she pointed out. "You could stay here for weeks and we wouldn't even know you were here. Besides, I can help you out taking care of my new niece."

Jake sighed. In a moment of desperation, he'd been selfish and he knew it. "You have a life, too, Erin," he pointed out. And he couldn't just impose on it because he found himself drowning.

Even when he was saying "yes"—tantamount to agreeing with her—her brother could be difficult. Actually, she should have expected this, Erin thought. But she was not about to allow Jake to talk himself out of coming back to Thunder Canyon. The bottom line was that Jake needed help and he *had* admitted it, however fleetingly.

"Family comes first," Erin reminded him. It was a principle she believed in with her whole heart, as did Corey. "Besides, I know a great babysitter who can pinch-hit when you need a break and I'm not available."

"A babysitter?" he echoed, saying the word with great disdain. "What, pay some teenager an arm and a leg while she's on her cell phone all night, twittering—"

"Tweeting," Erin corrected patiently. Even though she'd be the first to acknowledge how smart Jake was and how street-savvy he could be, her brother was a babe in the woods when it came to anything electronic.

"Whatever," he dismissed impatiently. "Or some old woman who smells like cats and falls asleep the second I close the front door?" he continued, then dismissed both with a "No, thanks."

"Calista Clifton isn't a teenager," Erin informed him of the young woman she was thinking of. "And she doesn't smell like cats. She's bright, cheerful and comes from a huge family, so she's no stranger to baby spit-up or diapers. You'll like her," Erin promised, for now not bothering to cite the young woman's other credits or mention her incredible work ethic. There was no response on the other end of the line. "Hello? Hello? Jake, are you there?"

His sister's voice roused him.

Jake realized that he was no longer looking at anything. Jerking, his eyes flew open.

It was at that moment that he realized that the water in the saucepan had almost boiled completely away and that he'd just dropped the phone receiver he'd been holding on the counter. He'd literally been asleep on his feet and the receiver had slipped out of his fingers.

Snatching it up, he pressed the receiver against his ear.

He didn't bother with an explanation, or apologizing. It would only give Erin more of an upper hand than he was already giving to her.

"Yeah, I'm still here," he answered.

Pressing his ear against the receiver, he tried to hold it in place using his head, neck and shoulder as he twisted the dial to the off position and moved the saucepan over to another burner.

Jake stifled a yelp as the metal handle he'd grabbed burned the center of his palm. The pain shot up to the roots of his hair.

Sucking in a steadying breath he pushed beyond the pain and said, "Okay, you talked me into it. I'll take a leave of absence and come up. You can get this Callous person—"

"Calista," Erin corrected.

"Yeah, her," he agreed. And then the policeman

inside him came out as he added, "But I want to interview her before I let her watch Marlie."

He heard his sister laugh. The warm sound was comforting. "I wouldn't have it any other way, big brother."

She didn't *really* need the money.

Between her summer internship for her cousin Bo Clifton, who just happened to be the mayor of Thunder Canyon, and her part-time job clerking at the Tattered Saddle, the local antique store, her finances, though not exactly overflowing, were in relatively decent shape. And what with the two jobs, free time wasn't exactly hanging heavily on Calista Clifton's hands.

But the fact of the matter was she really liked children, especially babies. And she also liked the feeling she got when she helped people. So it was hard for her to say no to the situation, as Erin Traub explained it to her, involving Erin's older brother because it actually encompassed both a baby *and* helping.

Even so, the thing that had ultimately cinched it for her was when Erin's brother, Jake Castro, walked into the room. She'd agreed to meet him and was sitting in Erin's spacious, sun-drenched living room when Jake came in holding his seven-month-old daughter in his arms.

If she was being honest, Calista would have had to admit that she'd noticed the baby belatedly. But that was only because Jake Castro was quite possibly the most incredibly handsome man who had ever crossed her path.

He was certainly handsome enough to cause her stomach muscles to tighten more than a little and for her palms to grow just the slightest bit damp. The latter hadn't happened to her since she was sixteen years old and had that wild crush on the captain of the football team—a guy who had turned out to be as empty and soulless as he was handsome.

Jake didn't look as if he was guilty of being empty or soulless. Not from the way he held that baby.

"It wouldn't be very often," Jake was saying to her after Erin had made the introductions and stated what they hoped her role would be in this situation, then slipped away so they could get acquainted. "Maybe once or twice a week at most, but—"

There was no need for him to try to convince her, Calista thought. He'd had her the second he'd walked into the room. Before he'd ever opened his mouth and she'd heard that baritone voice.

"Yes," Calista said with enthusiasm as she interrupted him.

Jake stopped, shifting his daughter to his other side. It was uncanny how Marlie always picked the wrong time to fuss. He looked at the young woman his sister had selected. Because he hadn't finished giving her the background information, he wasn't sure just what she was saying yes to.

"What?"

"Yes," Calista repeated with the same smiling, sunny enthusiasm.

"Yes?" He hadn't really even gotten into his sales

pitch yet, something that made him feel decidedly awkward because he wasn't accustomed to asking for anything, even something he had every intention of paying for. But this eleven-pound bundle in his arms had all the makings of being his own personal Waterloo.

Calista smiled. "Yes, I can be available for babysitting once or twice a week," she told him. "Or more often if the need arises." Her schedule was filled to overflowing, but she could find a way to make it work. She was utterly determined.

Having taken the job, Calista bit her lower lip, hesitating for a moment, wondering if she should say anything. The next moment she decided that if it was her in Jake's present position, she would appreciate being told.

She nodded at Jake's daughter. "Um, the baby—Marlie, is it?"

"That's right. Marlie," he confirmed. He wasn't all that crazy about the name. Had it been up to him, he would have named her something a little less fancy, but Maggie hadn't asked for his input in that. Maggie had been very specific about what she'd wanted—and didn't want—from him.

"Marlie just spat up on your shoulder," Calista told him.

"What?" He glanced down, embarrassed rather than annoyed.

"Here, let me take her," Calista offered. The next moment, she was very competently taking the baby into her own arms, drawing the infant away from the scene of the crime.

Even with his limited view, he could see that his daughter had spat up about a fourth of her last meal on the front—and shoulder—of his shirt. That left him with exactly one shirt that hadn't been christened with recycled baby food and/or formula.

He bit off the oath that automatically rose to his lips. He was still in training when it came down to that. But he was getting there.

Chapter Two

Calista didn't need to be a mind reader to figure out what the man standing in front of her with the newly stained shirt was thinking. When Erin called to ask about her availability to babysit occasionally in the evening, Jake's sister had given her a very brief summary of his present situation, including how he'd come to this point.

Although Erin hadn't gone into any specific detail, she assumed that Jake and Marlie's mother had been lovers, but that nothing formal had transpired, other than his name appearing on the birth certificate, which gave him legal guardianship to the infant.

However, all that was not any real business of hers. What she felt *was* her business was that Jake was obviously going to need all the help he could get to facilitate his getting accustomed to this brave new world of midnight feedings, formula runs and ever-increasing pile of stained shirts.

For starters, she thought, she could tell him how to deal with the last.

"If you give me your shirt, I can show you how to treat it," she said.

He looked at her, not quite sure what she was offering to do. "Treat it to what?"

Calista pressed her lips together, struggling not to laugh. "Not *to* something, *for* something. I can help you get rid of that stain," she explained. "Especially if I can get to it before it has a chance to really set in. Timing's important when it comes to things like that."

She could tell by his expression that he felt as if he was navigating in strange, uncharted waters. Most men, like her brothers, weren't into everyday, mundane complications. Clean clothes were a given, not something you needed to strive for.

And then she saw Jake shrug and then begin to unbutton his shirt.

She stared at him, stunned as she watched the shirt parting down the center of his chest. Her mouth turned to cotton. "What are you doing?"

His eyes narrowed in slight confusion. "I'm doing what you told me. You did say you wanted the shirt sooner than later, right?"

"Right," Calista murmured, her voice barely audible above a hushed whisper. Her soft brown eyes widened in wonder. She found it hard to tear them away from Jake's unveiling.

The man had rock-solid biceps and forearms. As for his abdomen, it looked as if it had been carefully sculptured by some divine artistic hand. The last time she'd seen a torso half as good, it had been in a photograph of one of the statues presently on display in a New York museum.

Having stripped off his shirt, Jake now held it out to Calista, exchanging the stained article of clothing for his daughter. As he nestled the infant against his chest, he couldn't help noting the somewhat dazed expression on the young woman's face. She was staring at him with a trace of disbelief in her wide eyes. Eyes, he noted, the color of warm chocolate.

"Something wrong?"

Calista blinked, then lowered her eyes. *Idiot,* she upbraided herself.

"No, nothing's wrong," she assured Jake a little too quickly. And then she added, "I'm just glad that Marlie didn't spit up on your jeans."

"Oh." Wasn't he supposed to give her the shirt now? "I thought you said it was better to work on a stain before it sets in, whatever that means."

If there were some kind of ritual to follow when it came to laundry, he hadn't a clue. He just threw everything in together and hoped for the best. Most of the time it worked. But that was before Marlie had come into his life.

Calista realized that she was staring at him again

and tore her eyes away, annoyed with herself. She was acting like some gawky juvenile, not like a twenty-two-year-old college graduate who fully intended to make her mark on the world.

"Right, I did." She focused her attention on the shirt in her hand and not on the man who'd been wearing it.

Whose warmth, she realized, she could still detect in the shirt's material. She felt her stomach tightening even more.

"Do you know if your sister has any lemon juice? Never mind," she negated her question in the next breath. "I'll go ask her."

And with that, she quickly left the room in search of Erin—as well as a couple of private minutes to herself. She needed to decelerate the rate of her pulse. which had gone into double time and was, even now, threatening to launch into triple time.

Calista found Erin at the front door, just about to leave to meet her husband. Jake's sister stopped when she saw her and then looked at the shirt she was holding in her hand.

"Boy—" Erin laughed "—I guess Jake was more desperate than I thought."

Calista shook her head, puzzled by the reference. "What?"

Erin gestured toward the shirt. "Well, Jake's obviously offering you the shirt off his back to get you to agree to take the job."

It took Calista almost a full beat to realize that Erin was kidding. The sight of Jake Castro's bare torso,

blended in with his low-slung jeans that hung precari-
ously on well-toned hips had rattled her more than she
was willing to admit even to herself.

"Very funny," she finally commented, then informed
Erin, "By the way, I'm taking the job."

Erin nodded. "I had a hunch." The sentence was accompanied by a wide—and relieved—grin. And then
she raised her eyebrows quizzically. Calista had obviously come looking for her and she rather doubted that
it had been just to inform her about her decision. She
looked back at the shirt the younger woman was holding. "Can I help you with something?"

But before Calista could say anything in response, a
deep voice right behind her answered the question for
her. "Calista says she can get rid of that stain for me—
that's actually my favorite shirt," he added in case Erin
wondered what all the fuss was about.

With Jake on the scene, Calista managed to snap out
of her mental reverie and found her tongue.

"Do you have any lemon juice?" she heard herself
asking Erin. "Soaking a stain in lemon juice usually
helps get the stubborn ones out," she told the other
woman.

That was news to Erin. But then, she really wasn't
all that domestic-minded. Yet.

"Good thing to know," Erin commented. She thought
for a moment before answering. "If we have any lemon
juice left, you'll find it in the refrigerator door, next to
the skim milk."

"I'll go look," Calista offered. "If you don't have any,

I can take the shirt home with me. I've got some lemon juice in the garage," she recalled.

That seemed like an odd thing to him to keep around. "You deal with a lot of spit-up during the course of the day?" Jake asked her.

"It doesn't just work on spit-up. It's good for getting out all sorts of stubborn stains," she explained as she made her way into the kitchen. "It's not a magic cure-all," she added, not wanting to mislead him. "But pretty nearly."

"Huh." He looked at the back of Calista's head for a split second, thinking she had pretty light brown hair, then commented, "Learn something every day."

Jake was right behind her and she was finding it more and more difficult to pretend that the man wasn't practically mouth-wateringly naked.

"That's life," Calista responded cheerfully. "One great big beautiful learning process."

My God, had she just uttered those inane words? Great. Now he probably thought she was some kind of dork, half Mary Poppins, half nerdy science geek. Or maybe even worse.

Erin opened the front door and quickly crossed the threshold. If she didn't leave now, there was no telling when she'd finally get the opportunity.

"Well, I'll leave you two to your chemistry experiment," Erin called out. "Let me know how it goes." She glanced one final time toward the young woman she'd brought over to meet Jake. "See you soon, Calista."

"Soon," Calista echoed with a nod, then looked at

Jake. "Unless you've changed your mind about hiring me as your sitter," she qualified.

She had a strong hunch that the man with the rock-hard chest had an acute aversion to women who gazed up at him with doe eyes. If he'd suddenly changed his mind about the arrangement, she didn't want to make it hard for him to tell her.

"Why would I change my mind?" he asked, mystified by her thinking. "You've definitely got the job," he assured her, then laughed. "I don't strip off my shirt for just anyone."

He was teasing the young woman, he realized. He hadn't done something like that—or anything else that was remotely lighthearted in nature—since he'd heard the awful news about Maggie getting shot.

He remembered his breath suddenly freezing in his lungs despite the warm weather—spring in New Orleans had a sticky dampness to it like no other place. And then, for weeks, he'd alternated between suppressed rage and numbness. He'd just assumed that things like teasing and smiling were behaviors he wouldn't be revisiting for a very long time to come and were, consequently, tucked away deep in his past.

Calista swallowed. Her mouth was inexplicably—not to mention incredibly—dry.

"I see," she replied, doing her best not to appear as affected as she was by this man.

At bottom, she tried to tell herself, individuals were all just a bunch of skin, tissues, organs and a great deal of water, haphazardly thrown together to form an arbitrary whole.

But, oh, the composition that had gone into making Jake Castro, she couldn't help thinking, growing warm all over again.

The next second, she was chastising herself for a second time. What was she, twelve? No, she was twenty-two, a grown woman, for heaven's sake, on a clearly cut path that was to ultimately lead to some sort of a position with the local government, possibly even an elected one. All of which meant that she couldn't afford to act like some starry-eyed juvenile just because the man standing next to her with the baby in his arms didn't appear to have an ounce of fat on him, even in his spare back pocket.

"Ah, lemon juice," she declared, spotting the little green plastic bottle with a picture of a lemon on it tucked away in the far end of the refrigerator door.

Saved by a grocery item, Calista thought, mocking herself sarcastically.

Bottle in hand, she looked around for somewhere she could continue this baptism-by-lemon-juice process. At first glance, nothing seemed to stand out.

"Do you know if your sister has a large plastic bowl she isn't using, or a sink I could take over for, say, a few hours?" she asked him hopefully.

The question caught Jake off guard. His eyes shifted to the shirt, then back to her. "This is going to take a few hours?"

"It might," Calista allowed, then qualified. "It can

be sooner and I'm not going to hang out here the entire time waiting," she promised, guessing that was probably what he was afraid of. "I just need somewhere I can leave your shirt to soak without having it disturbed or in the way."

For the time being, until he could find his own place, Erin had insisted that he remain with her and her husband. When he and Marlie had arrived and Corey had chimed in with the same invitation—and as far as Jake could tell, his brother-in-law was actually sincere—Jake found himself agreeing. Secretly, he had to admit that he was relieved. It was always easier looking for a place if he had somewhere that served as his home base until he found something suitable for himself and the baby.

"There's a bathroom off the guest room that I'm using," he volunteered. "You could leave my shirt soaking in the sink."

Calista grinned, nodding. "Sounds like a plan." She gestured vaguely toward the front of the house. "Lead the way."

Marlie made a gurgling noise as her father turned on his heel. The next moment, Calista saw him shiver. She guessed at what had happened even before he told the baby, "At least this time there's nothing for you to get dirty." Marlie had spat up on his bare shoulder.

With that, Jake led the way to the stairs.

No doubt about it, Calista thought as she followed behind him and walked up the stairs to his room, the man looked good coming *and* going.

There went her stomach again, contracting into a knot.

Get a grip, she ordered herself. *The man needs someone to help him out, not to drool all over him. He's already got the latter covered.*

When they came to the landing, Jake brought her over to the second door on the right. The door was closed. He opened it, then walked in and nodded toward the bathroom located over in the far corner of the room. There were four other guest rooms in the large house, but this one was the largest. Erin had told him that she thought this would be more suitable to his needs, especially with the baby.

"Right in through there," he told Calista. He pointed in the direction of the bathroom as he stopped by the bureau. Opening the top drawer, he pulled out a handkerchief and wiped away the latest deposit of baby drool from his shoulder. That done, he absently shoved the handkerchief into his back pocket.

Setting Marlie down in her portacrib for a moment, Jake went over to the closet. He was still in the process of unpacking, but there were a few shirts already hanging there. He grabbed the one closest to him, a blue pullover that, once on, brought out the color of his eyes more intensely.

His stained shirt still clutched in her hand, Calista forced herself to look away and head toward the bathroom. She couldn't help but notice that the room looked as if it'd had an encounter with a tornado, and lost.

"Still unpacking?" Calista asked, raising her voice so that he could hear her.

"Still hunting for things," he amended. "Well, I'm

decent again," he said to his daughter after he'd pulled on the new shirt. "Try to keep your lunch down for at least a few minutes," he urged her, picking up the baby again.

Marlie cooed in response, as if she understood him and was telling him that she'd do her best to try.

The noise made him smile. Funny how outwardly perfectly insignificant things like a sound coming from a seven-month-old infant could make him feel so warm inside. He supposed this was what being a father was all about, celebrating the small, personal things that no one else was privy to or could begin to comprehend.

He looked over toward the bathroom. The woman he'd just agreed to allow to watch over his daughter was still in there, but he wasn't hearing any sounds.

"Let's go see what's up," he said to his daughter as he crossed to the other end of the bedroom. "So how's it coming?" he asked Calista, raising his voice.

Calista glanced at him over her shoulder. He was standing in the doorway of the bathroom, once again holding Marlie in his arms, and mercifully wearing a shirt again.

Now if only that fact would register with her racing pulse and make it settle down, she thought.

"It's coming along," she repeated.

To prove her point, she picked up the shirt and held it up over the sink to allow him to see for himself. She'd filled the basin with a little water to dilute the concentrated lemon juice and it was dripping down as she raised the shirt for his perusal. The spot that Marlie had branded with a gooey, milky-white substance was actually growing fainter.

"Like I said," she repeated, pleased, "sometimes it takes a little longer than other times. But it looks like you won't have to throw this one away."

He joined her at the sink for a closer look. It really was fading, he thought, impressed.

"So that's all I have to do?" he asked, his eyes shifting to look at her. "Just pour lemon juice on it and let it soak? Because I've got about ten shirts that really need work," he confessed. "None of them would really come clean, even after I threw them into the washing machine a couple of times." He was on the verge of throwing them all out. Tossing out shirts after wearing them only once or twice wasn't exactly something he could afford to do indefinitely.

Calista looked a little skeptical as she asked him, "When you washed your shirts, you didn't have the setting on hot, did you?"

Damned if he knew. "The machine has settings?" he asked.

"Why don't you pile them up for me and I'll take a look at your shirts the next time you have me over to watch Marlie?" she suggested.

Initially he had balked at asking for help or letting anyone know that he wasn't up to handling this situation he found himself in. But after closer scrutiny, maybe this wasn't going to be such a bad deal after all, Jake thought. If this cheerful woman with the sparkling brown eyes and endless brown hair could save his shirts as well as help him save his sanity, she was clearly worth her weight in gold.

"Sounds good to me," he responded to the suggestion with feeling.

Yes, Calista thought, unable to contain her smile any longer, it certainly did.

Chapter Three

"You're late."

Jasper Fowler bit off the words as he glared at Calista from beneath shaggy gray-and-white eyebrows.

Just coming in, Calista eased the door to the Tattered Saddle antique shop closed behind her. If Fowler expected her to flinch at his obvious displeasure, he was going to be sorely disappointed, she thought. Growing up amid seven brothers and sisters had long since taught her how to hold her ground and stand up for herself. It was either that or suddenly find herself getting plowed under and lost in the shuffle.

So far, she'd never once gotten lost in the shuffle.

"I'm on time," Calista corrected pleasantly, deliberately pointing to the closest clock to her on the wall.

Currently, there were several clocks on display, all

hanging on the shop walls, all antiques, all fashioned with a decidedly Western flavor. And each and every one of them testified to the fact that she, and not the crotchety, cantankerous elderly owner of the store, was right. She was right on time.

With a frame that resembled nothing if not an animated question mark, his shoulders hunched in so far that they appeared to be almost touching one another, Fowler moved past her and grumbled, "Well, you would have been late in another minute."

As was his habit, he refused to give in or concede the point. If asked, no one in town could recollect *ever* hearing the old man admit that he was wrong—about anything.

"But I didn't take another minute," Calista countered cheerfully. "So I'm here on time."

In her own way, she was just as stubborn as the old man she was working for this summer. Beneath it all, she wanted to think that the man rather enjoyed sparring with her, enjoyed the challenge of having someone who didn't cave in to him. Everyone else, she'd noted, always backed away, considering a verbal bout with the man just a waste of time and energy.

Maybe she was wrong, she thought, picking up the ancient feather duster he required she use every day to dust the eclectic collection of memorabilia he housed within the old shop's four walls. But in complying with his specific instructions and using the duster, Calista couldn't help but feel that all she was accomplishing was pushing the dust around, ineffectively moving it from one spot to another and then back again the next day.

But the pay was the same whether she eliminated the dust or just gave it another place to stay, so she had given up trying to introduce a few basic improvements into the daily routine. Fowler, she'd quickly discovered, was a stickler for adhering to routines, to all but worshipping the status quo.

She'd learned her first week here that it was pointless to try to point out the benefits of doing anything new or different.

But then, she reasoned, if Fowler had been opened to new things, he probably wouldn't be dealing with items that were older than he was.

"When I finish dusting out here, if there aren't any customers, maybe I'll just go dust the storeroom," she volunteered.

Although she'd brought along a couple of books to review, books that promised to help her get a better handle on her internship at the mayor's office, she really didn't like being idle for any stretch of time and because Fowler *was* paying her—minimum wage to be sure, but it was still her salary—her first efforts should be to do something worthwhile in the antique store.

About to shuffle off into the very same storeroom she was proposing to clean, Fowler stopped short and turned around to glare at her.

"No," he all but shouted, then struggled to regain his monotone composure. "I already told you to stay out of there."

He'd told her that the very first day she'd worked here. At the time she'd thought the edict was just fueled by his myriad of idiosyncrasies.

"I know, but I thought maybe you'd like to have me straighten things up in there, maybe do an inventory for you," she proposed.

"Don't need no inventory," Fowler retorted. "I know everything that's in there and where it is if I need to get at it. I don't need some eager beaver messing things up with her own damn system that makes no sense to nobody on God's green earth but her."

He was really getting heated about it and she couldn't help wondering why. She'd glanced into the storeroom once in passing and it was just a dark storage space as far as she could see.

"Okay, I won't go in there," she surrendered, at the same time trying to figure out just what it was that the old man was trying to protect. Most likely, it was nothing, but he certainly was behaving peculiarly—even more so than usual. Every time she mentioned the storeroom, he acted, in her opinion, as if she was trying to break into the U.S. Mint and he was its only defender.

But then, she reasoned, she'd known what the old man was like when she'd initially answered his want ad and interviewed for the job. Everyone in town— her family included—had warned her about going to work for "crazy ol' Jasper Fowler." And everyone from around the area knew about the legend.

Knew how, according to the legend, Fowler had once driven cross-country with a coffin rattling around in the back of his pickup truck. Moreover, the same legend claimed that there'd been a rotting corpse in that coffin, supposedly the remains of a woman who had once jilted him.

Over time other identities had been assigned to the so-called decaying cross-country traveler. Some said it was a business partner who had tried to cheat him out of the profits of their business. Others said that there were two bodies in there, his late wife and the infant son she'd given birth to minutes before both she and the baby had died.

That, at least, would explain his winning personality.

As for her, Calista figured that because the old man *was* so eccentric, Fowler invited these kinds of stories to be made up about him, maybe even reveled in them and that, ultimately, none of it was true.

Although, if it *was* true she supposed that might be a good reason why Fowler wouldn't allow anyone but him to enter the storeroom. That might be where he was keeping the legendary coffin.

Stop it, she told herself. *You're smarter than that. There's no coffin. It's all just a bunch of fabrication about an odd old man.*

She heard the front door open. The next second she heard the bell attached to it ring, announcing the entrance of another person into the store.

Having already walked into the storeroom, Fowler poked his head out to see who had come in. The etched-in frown on his stubble-laden face seemed to deepen as his small eyes focused on the woman who had just come into his shop.

Recognizing her, he challenged Erin Traub. "You here to buy anything today?"

Erin knew how to play the game. "I might be," she answered evasively.

Fowler allowed a dismissive sound to escape his lips as he waved his hand at Erin's words. "No, you ain't. You got five minutes to talk to the girl and then you go," he ordered. "And you," he said, shifting his hawk-like intense gaze to Calista, "consider this your break, you hear?"

"Yes, sir," Calista answered, inclining her head with a formal little bow, as if he was some small far-from-benevolent despot.

Uttering another dismissive noise, Fowler withdrew back into the storeroom.

Erin looked at the younger woman she'd come to see in disbelief. "How can you stand it, working for Old Man Fowler? He's so rude."

"I've had practice dealing with foul moods. When you've got seven siblings, there's always someone who's bound to be in a snit—or worse," she added with a care-less shrug. "And besides, it's not exactly like I don't need the money," she confessed. At twenty-two, she'd just graduated, but that didn't mean that all that strug-gling was behind her. A great deal of it was just up ahead. She was currently living at home to save as much money as she could, but it was still slow-going. "I've got school loans to pay off and other expenses to juggle as well. Right now, I can't afford to be picky." Besides, she added silently, afraid of being overheard, Fowler was harmless.

"Is that why you agreed to babysit for my brother?" Erin asked her.

She'd stopped by to get her friend's take on working for her brother and to make sure that Calista didn't decide to suddenly change her mind and tell Jake that she'd had second thoughts about agreeing to babysit for him. Dealing with an infant could be draining. Especially after having had to put up with a Neanderthal despot like Fowler.

"Oh no," Calista said with feeling, "I'm more than happy to take the job. I think that Marlie's really adorable."

Erin laughed. She had fallen in love with her niece at first sight, but she had to admit that there were drawbacks. "For a child who never sleeps, she's wonderful." Erin raised her slender shoulders and then let them drop. "At least it feels that way. Our bedroom is just one door down from Jake's room. I can hear him pacing the floor with her at all hours. That baby cries every night."

"Well, yes, that's not unusual. They do that for a while," Calista assured her. "But that eventually changes and they sleep through the night. For the record, babies don't learn to manipulate their parents until they're a few years old."

Erin sighed, wondering how she would measure up when the time came to have a baby of her own. Right now, it seemed almost daunting to even think about.

"You sound a lot more knowledgeable about how to handle things than I am."

Calista shrugged off the compliment. "I come from a really big family," she pointed out. "Somewhere along the line, I started taking care of my younger brothers and sisters. Suddenly, I was the expert when it came to changing diapers, feeding and burping. The funny thing is, I don't really mind, so I can't complain. The truth of the matter is," she freely admitted, "I kind of like it."

"You don't have to sell me," Erin assured her with feeling. "I actually just stopped by to find out if there's anything I can do to make the experience better for you."

Several things popped up in her mind, none of which she could have ventured to say out loud. All of them concerned Jake Castro. The very thought of him made her feel warm, a reaction she did her best to stifle. It wasn't something she could readily explain to the man's sister.

Instead, she guessed at the reason behind Erin's impromptu field trip to the antique shop, and her. "Don't worry, Erin, I said I'd babysit and I'm not going to change my mind."

"Good." Erin released a large sigh, then immediately asked, "Are you busy tomorrow night?"

Calista hadn't expected to be asked to babysit so soon. She looked at Jake's sister in surprise.

"Tomorrow," she repeated, thinking for a second. "I was just planning to do a little dry reading on government procedures so I don't come across like some empty-headed little intern. I don't want people to think that Cousin Bo's guilty of nepotism, although technically, I suppose he is." Their connection was distant, but they were still family. "Why? Is Jake going out tomorrow night? He didn't mention anything to me about it during the interview."

She would have assumed that he would have right after telling her that she had the job. Had something come up, or had he just held back for some reason of his own?

The smile that rose to Erin's lips was a self-satisfied one. "That's because my big brother doesn't know he's going out yet."

"You're having him kidnapped?" Calista guessed drily.

To her surprise, Erin answered the quip seriously. "In a manner of speaking. I want Corey and Jake to have a guys' night out."

She might not have a whole lot of experience beyond her academic one, but that struck Calista as rather unusual.

"You haven't been married all that long," she recalled, then marveled, "Boy, talk about an understanding wife."

Amused, Erin set the other woman straight. "Don't stick wings on me yet, Calista. There's a reason for my shipping those two out of the house. I want a clear playing field so that I can help Corey's sister get ready for her date."

It was a small enough town to keep up on the various activities of the locals. Corey's baby sister Rose was, like her brothers, a recent transplant to Thunder Canyon. As such, she didn't know all that many people yet.

Calista greeted the news with surprise. "I didn't know that Rose was dating."

Even though they were alone in the front room of the shop, Erin still drew closer and lowered her voice. "That's just the problem, she hasn't been and she's really nervous about going out."

To Calista, going out on a date was just an extension of talking. But she supposed she could see why it might make someone else a little nervous. If she were about to go out with Jake, there might be more than one or two butterflies involved.

"So who's the lucky guy she's going out with?" she asked Erin.

Erin paused for a moment. This wouldn't have been her first choice, but it certainly was going to be a great way for Rose to get her feet wet again. "It's Nick Pritchett."

"Bo's brother-in-law?" Calista asked, surprised.

The name belonged to yet another one of her distant relatives, this one being really distant. On the stocky side and more than a little opinionated, Nick Pritchett was one relative she certainly didn't mind keeping distant.

Erin nodded, deliberately masking her own thoughts on the matter. "The very same."

Calista laughed shortly. "Well, you can tell Rose she

doesn't have anything to be nervous about. All she has to do is show up and breathe. From what I hear, Nick'll take it from there and do all the talking. And I do mean *all*. The man really does like to hear the sound of his own voice."

There was no point in pretending that this was a good thing. Erin surrendered the charade.

"Well, she has to start somewhere," she said helplessly.

At least she hadn't been the one to arrange this, Erin thought. Nick had asked Rose out and her sister-in-law, responding to some sort of newly instituted panic that she was liable to be alone for the rest of her life, had jumped at the chance.

Picking up on the less-than-thrilled note in Erin's voice, Calista's inner optimism suddenly rallied and rose to the surface.

"I'm sure it'll be fine," she told the other woman encouragingly.

Blowing out a breath, Erin nodded again, more to herself than to Calista. She needed to deal with what was, not with what she wished would be. And Rose needed to learn how to take baby steps. Whatever her sister-in-law might be thinking about her future with Nick, this was really just a practice run, getting her prepared for when a more suitable man came along.

"And you'll be there tomorrow?" she asked Calista.

Calista smiled and nodded, ignoring her own butterflies when she thought of seeing Jake Castro again.

"I'll be there tomorrow. What time do you want me to show up?"

Erin quickly calculated optimal time for everything to take place. Corey would be available around five-thirty or so. "Six o'clock okay?"

Six was when she left the mayor's office. She really didn't want to ask for a half-hour time-off so soon into her internship. "Six-thirty would be better."

She wasn't inflexible. "Fine. Six-thirty," Erin agreed.

There was just one more thing Calista wanted to know before tomorrow night. "You are going to tell your brother about his 'guys' night out' before I get there, right? I mean, he's not going to be surprised when I just show up on your doorstep, is he? I wouldn't want the guy thinking I'm stalking him."

When they were growing up, Jake was the brother beset by females, all eager for his attention. All in all, Erin was fairly sure that by now, Jake was accustomed to having a woman turn up on the doorstep, looking for him.

"Don't worry, I'm telling Corey about it tonight and I'll have him twist Jake's arm. He won't say no to Corey," Erin assured her. She could see that Calista was wondering why she wanted to get rid of both her husband and her brother for the evening because Rose's "big date" didn't really affect either one of them. "I don't want either one of them hanging around while Rose gets ready. You know what brothers are like. She doesn't need to be teased unmercifully about this. She's already nervous enough as it is. I just want her to be as confident and poised as she can be under the circumstances."

To Calista, it was a case of much ado about nothing, but she kept that to herself. Anything else she might have said would have to wait. Fowler came shuffling in from the back just then and peered at Erin, scowling.

"You still here?" It was more of an accusation than a question.

Erin shifted, turning toward the door. "I was just leaving, Mr. Fowler," she informed him. With effort, she pasted a wide smile on her face for Calista's sake. She didn't want the old man taking Calista to task because she'd overstayed her welcome.

If she thought it might get her on Fowler's good side, she'd wasted her time. It made no difference.

"Don't let the door hit you on the way out," he retorted, pointing a bony finger toward the door.

Most of the time she could just turn a deaf ear to the old man's rudeness, but when it was aimed at someone else, it really irritated her. Walking Erin to the door, she debated that perhaps it was time for her to start looking for another job. It was just a matter of time before she couldn't hold her tongue around Mr. Personality. Eventually, she was going to put him in his place.

"I'll see you tomorrow night," Calista promised. She saw pity in Erin's eyes as the woman glanced toward Fowler. It didn't take a genius to figure out what Erin was thinking.

"Maybe the mayor can give you a raise," Erin suggested in a whisper as she crossed the threshold.

"That would *really* be nepotism," Calista said with a laugh.

"I'm not paying you to stand there, jawing the day away," Fowler informed her, raising his voice so that people in the street outside could hear him.

"No, you're not," Calista agreed, forcing herself to sound cheerful.

Closing the door, she looked at her part-time employer. In truth, she felt sorry for the old man. He obviously had no friends and he alienated almost everyone he came in contact with. She had no idea how he even made a living. Since she'd started working at the shop, there had been only a handful of customers and maybe five sales. Of course, she was only here part-time, so maybe the bulk of the sales were conducted when she wasn't around. For his sake, she hoped so. Otherwise, she couldn't see how he would be able to manage to stay in business for any length of time.

But that, she reminded herself, wasn't any of her concern. Instead, she focused on the fact that she was going to be seeing Jake again tomorrow night, however briefly.

The butterflies in her stomach returned, bringing friends.

Chapter Four

Jake really didn't feel like going out for dinner that night. There were a number of rentals he'd circled in the newspaper that he wanted to review. Beyond that, he'd just planned a quiet evening getting in some bonding time with his daughter. This being a father thing was all still pretty new to him.

But when Corey had asked him to go out and grab some dinner with him, Jake felt that he couldn't very well turn down his brother-in-law, not when Corey and Erin had taken him in like this with open arms. At the very least saying no to Corey's invitation could come off as being ungrateful.

To win him over, Corey had even told him that he could be the one to pick the restaurant—as if he was familiar with the area, Jake thought.

But, on the other hand, going out would serve as a mental diversion for him and right about now, he needed to be diverted. *And* he really needed to put pressing, serious matters out of his mind.

Jake glanced at the letter he'd balled up and tossed on the coffee table earlier. The letter that had been tracking his whereabouts and had finally caught up with him here.

Maybe he shouldn't have left a forwarding address at the post office in New Orleans, he thought. But then, if he'd just up and completely disappeared, he might have been charged with kidnapping by the people who'd sent him this letter. He was certain that by now, Maggie's parents had gotten themselves a lawyer to contest their daughter's final decision.

He knew that Mr. and Mrs. O'Shea maintained that Maggie hadn't been in her right mind on her deathbed when she'd given custody of their little girl to him, especially because up until that point, she'd insisted that he have nothing to do with raising the baby, that the responsibility was all hers.

But nothing in the world was going to make him not honor his late partner's request. Hell, even if she hadn't asked him to take care of their little girl, he would have been there to watch over Marlie. He couldn't imagine himself doing anything else.

He might not know what the hell he was doing, but those were just details. They'd work themselves out. The main thing was that Marlie was his blood, his child. He hadn't thought the feeling would be so strong, but the moment he'd first laid eyes on her, it had been there, full-blown and vital. Marlie was his and he intended to do whatever it took to hang on to her. If that meant having to go into hiding someday, so be it.

As a police officer, he considered himself exceptionally law-abiding, but this was his child and there was no way on God's green earth he was about to just turn her over to anyone, even her own grandparents. When she'd gotten pregnant, Maggie had told him stories about her childhood, about how almost fanatically strict her father had been, so much so that she ran away from home the moment she turned eighteen.

Someone like that wasn't going to get his hands on Marlie, Jake thought. The little girl belonged with him. And he was doing his best to become the competent father she deserved.

Granted he was still tangled up in the learning curve, but he was getting there. Slowly but surely, he was getting there. He figured that by the time Marlie was in her teens, he'd have it all down pat. With any luck.

"You probably won't want to have anything to do with me by then," he told the infant he was holding tucked against his chest with one arm.

He could remember Erin when she'd been a teenager. She'd wanted to have nothing to do with either of her parents. Instead, she'd been hell-bent to try her own wings and be independent. There were arguments practically every day.

It wasn't that their parents had been particularly strict—not anything like what Maggie had said about her father—it was just that Erin had been a stubborn mule, determined to have things her own way. He was fairly certain that Erin's unruly behavior was why their father—and their mother—had prematurely gone gray.

"You wouldn't do that to me, would you, Marlie?" he asked out loud, looking down at the tiny round face. Cornflower-blue eyes stared back at him, wide and intense, as if the infant was hanging on every syllable that he uttered. She might have Maggie's red hair, but she had his eyes, he thought, pleased. "You wouldn't turn my hair prematurely gray because you wanted to stay out all night doing God knows what with God knows who, right, Marlie? You're my good little girl."

"I don't know, Daddy, I think you might look good in gray hair," a high-pitched voice—obviously pretending to give him an answer as Marlie—said behind him.

Caught off guard, Jake swung around, only to see Calista walking into the living room. She flashed an apologetic grin at him.

He looked startled. Not when he'd turned around, but when their eyes had made contact. Why?

"Sorry, didn't mean to spook you," she told him, crossing to the sofa where he stood. "I just couldn't resist."

While he obviously knew it wasn't Marlie talking—he thought she was special, but not *that* special—he'd assumed it was Erin who was pretending to answer him as his daughter. Seeing Calista standing there instead had temporarily thrown him off.

He was about to ask her what she was doing here, but

because this wasn't his house, the question would undoubtedly come across as sounding rude and he didn't want that.

So instead he asked, "Are you here to see Erin?"

"Well, this is awkward," Calista said, more to herself than to him. She saw Jake's eyebrows draw together over his electric-blue eyes in a silent question. Trapped, Calista had no choice but to explain what had prompted her comment. "Erin said she was going to tell you."

So far, this wasn't getting any clearer. "Tell me what?"

Belatedly she realized that she'd certainly put her foot into her mouth. Well, might as well make room for the other one as well, Calista thought philosophically.

"That you and Corey are going out together for dinner." She deliberately refrained from referring to the evening as a "guys' night out," thinking he might take offense at that.

"I already know that. Corey already asked me to come with him." He was still unclear what she was doing here. "But how do you figure into it?"

And then suddenly, alarms went off in Jake's head. There was nothing that he hated more than being set up on a "blind" date. Had Erin decided that he needed female companionship to get over Maggie's tragic death and that this attractive little slip of a girl was going to be it? Was Callie—no, Calista—supposed to be his date?

There was no other way but to put it to her bluntly. "Are you coming with us?"

The question, coming out of the blue, stunned her. Was this Jake's way of asking her out on a date?

Don't get carried away. Men like Jake didn't beat around the bush; they asked directly. And they don't ask women like you.

She was pretty sure that to someone like Jake, she came across as a life-size Barbie doll despite her medium-brown hair. It was up to her to prove that she had far more substance than that.

"No, I'm staying here and watching Marlie for you," she explained simply. She made eye contact with the infant, thinking how much the baby's eyes looked like Jake's. "Aren't I, Marlie?" As if in response, a bubble emerged from the infant's rosebud mouth. Tickled, she looked up at Jake. "I think that's a 'yes.'"

He still didn't understand. "Why are you watching Marlie?" he wanted to know. "Why isn't my sister doing it?"

"Because I'm going to be busy helping Rose get ready, that's why," Erin answered, walking into the room.

After letting Calista in, she'd rushed upstairs to tell Corey to get a move on, then come back down to check on Jake. He'd obviously gotten his signals crossed, she thought.

Jake turned to look at his sister. "Get ready for what?"

She wasn't about to undertake a long explanation. Rose was going to be here any minute. She wanted

Corey and her brother to be gone by then. "Never mind, you just go with Corey and have a good time."

As if on cue, Marlie began to wail. "Here, give her to me," Calista urged, taking the squalling infant from him.

It wasn't that he felt he could do anything better than this confident young woman his sister had brought to his attention; it was just that he was suddenly feeling very protective and parental toward his daughter. He didn't want to just leave her like this. What if this wasn't just a regular crying jag? What if Marlie was hurting for some reason?

"I don't know," Jake hedged. "Maybe I should stay." He turned to look at Erin. "I'm sure that Corey will take a rain check."

Suddenly Erin moved behind him. Placing her hands on his back, she began to push him toward the front door. Hard. "It's raining right now, Jake," she told him firmly. "Go. Just go." It was an order.

Surprisingly strong, Erin managed to make some headway with him toward the door.

Erin had definitely piqued his curiosity. "You having some kind of an all-girl party here or something?" he wanted to know.

"Right," she quickly agreed. "I'm having an all-girl party and you're not invited. Now go. Shoo."

"Someone's having a party?" Corey asked as he came down to the bottom of the stairs.

She was out of time and out of patience. Hands on her hips, she looked from one annoying male to the other.

"It's going to be your funeral if you two don't get out of here."

Holding his ground a minute longer, Corey stood just shy of the threshold and looked at his new brother-in-law. "She always been this pushy?"

"She has for as long as I've known her," Jake deadpanned.

Because he and Jake had just crossed the threshold and were standing outside the front door, it was all but slammed shut behind them. Corey laughed. "Subtle, isn't she?"

Jake merely shook his head in response. "Not that I ever noticed."

Corey led the way to his car. Generally laid-back in most matters, he still preferred being the one doing the driving when he was in a vehicle.

"So," he said as he got in on the driver's side and waited for his brother-in-law to get in and buckle up before turning on the ignition. "You know where you want to go on this official 'guys' night out' Erin's sending us on?"

Jake had given the matter a little thought and was pleased to have come up with a name. "Well, I'm kind of partial to barbecue ribs. What do you think of going to Lipsmackin' Ribs?"

He'd remembered that he'd driven by the restaurant a couple of times while driving into town to run some errands and the establishment had looked rather inviting. He'd even caught a tempting whiff when he'd passed by with his car windows opened. Best of all, it was close by.

Shifting slightly, he glanced at Corey, waiting for the other man to either approve or disapprove of his choice.

Prompted by his sense of loyalty, Corey's first inclination was to veto his brother-in-law's suggestion. The restaurant Jake had just mentioned was one that was in direct competition with his cousin DJ's place, DJ's Rib Shack.

When he didn't say anything, Jake looked at Corey's expression. His brother-in-law looked less than thrilled. "No good?" he guessed.

"Oh, what the hell?" Corey said gamely. Maybe he could find out something to help DJ's business. It never hurt to scope out the competition. "Might not be a bad idea to check it out, see what they've got." When Jake looked a little puzzled, it occurred to him that Jake might not know what he was talking about. "My cousin owns a rib joint," he explained. "You've probably driven past it. DJ's Rib Shack."

Offhand, the name meant nothing to Jake. But he hadn't exactly been playing the newly transplanted tourist. Now he understood why Corey had hesitated when he'd mentioned the other restaurant. "We can go there instead, if you'd rather."

With his type A personality, Corey was used to taking charge. But he didn't want Erin's brother to think he was the type to throw his weight around just because he felt he could. Because Jake had brought up the other restaurant, he wanted to be fair about this. And when all was said and done, it could work out to DJ's advantage if he went here.

"No, the place you mentioned's a little closer and besides, like I said, it wouldn't hurt to check out the competition for my cousin. Unofficially, of course," he added with a wink.

"Like industrial spies?" Jake asked. It seemed like the simple guys' night out had turned into an exercise in low-level espionage.

Corey laughed. "Not exactly, but close. You game?"

"Sure, why not?"

"That's what I like to hear," Corey declared, gunning his engine. And with that, they sped away.

Lipsmackin' Ribs turned out to be exceedingly popular. The restaurant was all but packed, despite the fact that it was a weekday evening.

At least part of the reason, Jake was fairly certain, had nothing to do with the fact that the tantalizing aroma of the barbecued ribs were wafting into the parking lot, snaring unsuspecting passersby with the promise of a little bit of gastronomic heaven.

Superior or not, the ribs came in a distant second behind the allure of the servers, every single one female with a capital *F.* They were slender, attractive women, and every last one of them had incredibly long legs no matter how tall or petite she was. Each woman wore four-inch heels, solid royal blue short shorts and either royal blue or white T-shirts cut short to reveal lots of belly, embossed with the restaurant's logo: a pair of wide, smiling, satisfied lips. The results were that no testosterone-laden customer was really all that aware of the meal he was eating. Their attention was definitely distracted, to say the least.

Gorgeous though the waitresses were, Jake found himself measuring the women up against the perky babysitter with smiling eyes who had so recently come into his life. He found the other women taking second place. *Whoa,* he thought. *Not the route to take.*

Searching for a distraction, Jake found himself all but mesmerized by the rhythmic sway of their waitress's hips as she walked away after bringing them their order. She'd been a little flustered and had almost dropped the tray when she'd returned with their food. The server, an extremely pretty girl named Jeannette according to the name tag pinned to her chest, had explained with a nervous laugh that she hadn't been at this too long.

Jake found himself the one doing the talking. When he glanced toward his brother-in-law, he saw that Corey was deliberately *not* staring at the young woman.

He waited until the woman had walked away and then said to Corey, "You know, it *is* all right to look." His brother-in-law appeared to be the only breathing male whose eyes were not firmly fastened on one server or another. Several men at the various tables scattered around them were just sitting back, openly enjoying the local talent walking by. "You married my sister, you weren't pronounced dead."

His attention focused on eating, Corey glanced up

from his meal. "I meant what I said about checking the place out."

"Doesn't that encompass more than just what's on the menu?" Jake wanted to know.

Corey knew what his brother-in-law was driving at. "Maybe they hired all these nubile, lovely young hostesses to distract customers from the fact that their ribs might be second rate."

Jake shrugged, open to any theory. But from what he'd just sampled, the ribs could stand on their own without that sort of help. "That's one idea," Jake agreed.

After sampling a few more pieces, Corey was forced to admit the ribs were as "lip smacking" as they'd been advertised. With the barbecued meat all but falling off the bone, the ribs were incredibly delicious.

And familiar-tasting, Corey decided after consuming most of his order.

He looked at Jake, a note of vindicating triumph in his voice. "These ribs taste just like the ones that DJ makes," he told his brother-in-law. Anger warred with indignation. "They must have gotten hold of DJ's recipe somehow."

Although he wanted to be supportive, Jake saw no real reason for Corey to make that sort of an accusation. "Maybe it's just a coincidence that they taste like the ones your cousin makes. I mean, just how many different ways can you really make barbecue ribs?" he asked his brother-in-law.

Corey frowned slightly. Spoken like a man who obviously didn't know his way around a barbecue grill, Corey thought.

"A lot," he answered patiently, cutting Jake some slack because he was new.

He could hear Corey's restrained annoyance. "I'm not trying to get into an argument here, Corey. But don't you think there's just the slightest chance that you're reading too much into this?"

"Maybe," Corey allowed grudgingly, but he really didn't think so.

DJ needed to get out here, Corey decided. DJ was the only one qualified enough to know if this was just a coincidence, or if the ribs were an exact duplicate of the recipe that he'd come up with.

With effort, Corey forced a smile to his lips and concentrated on just having a good time with his brother-in-law whose company he really did enjoy.

And all things considered, it was rather nice being able to talk to the man without his having a crying baby on his arm, no matter how cute Erin maintained that baby was.

Chapter Five

Rose Traub stood looking at her reflection in the wood-framed, full-length, three-sided mirror in her sister-in-law's master suite.

The five-foot-five blue-eyed redhead knew that Erin had said she looked beautiful, but all she saw when she looked into the mirror was a scared, nervous-looking young woman staring back at her.

And despite all the effort that had been put into her makeover in the last ninety minutes, she still wasn't happy with what she saw.

Her hair was too wavy, her eyes too blue. She'd been too much of a tomboy growing up, trying to hold her own with her five older brothers, and it showed, she thought in despair. She felt she didn't have a feminine bone in her body.

And she certainly didn't look sexy.

Even so, she was a born romantic and at this point in her life, she was desperate to find someone to love, desperate to find her very own happily-ever-after. Like Corey had.

"You *do* look very pretty," Erin told her again, breaking into the nervous silence that was all but physically emanating from her sister-in-law. Bright-eyed and eager, Rose still really had no self-confidence to speak of.

"I'm thirty years old," Rose lamented, giving voice to the mantra that kept playing over and over in her head. She met Erin's eyes in the mirror. "Do you know what that is in dog years?"

"Too old," Calista replied matter-of-factly. Erin, in an attempt to build up Rose's confidence, had asked Calista to join them. The younger woman all but radiated a positive, optimistic manner and Erin hoped that it would somehow rub off on Corey's baby sister. "If you *were* a dog, you would have been dead by now. Instead, you're a lovely, poised young woman who any man would be thrilled to be able to take out on the town."

"Thrilled?" Rose echoed, turning around to look at the woman who was almost a decade younger than she was. The way she said the word reminded Calista of a flower that was desperately seeking a life-sustaining drink of water.

"Thrilled," Calista repeated with conviction. Out of the corner of her eye, she saw Erin looking at her with noticeable approval. Rose, apparently, needed a great deal more encouragement. Calista went to work. "And why not? You're young, beautiful and a very competent professional."

She'd heard that in public, when dealing with clients, Rose was the picture of confidence and competence. She was in charge of handling the public relations end of the family oil business. Just recently, she'd also taken on publicity and communications tasks for Cousin Bo in his capacity as the town's mayor. It was the latter position that had allowed her to get to know Rose a little better.

It also allowed her to see that there seemed to be a complete world of difference between the public Rose and the private one. It was almost as if they weren't the same person. Calista was certain that it was because Rose wanted a relationship and all that it entailed so much that she was getting in her own way.

"Listen, before Nick gets here, could you just—" Rose was about to ask Erin for some tips as to what to talk about on her date, but just then, the doorbell rang.

"Too late," Erin declared. She'd had Rose tell Nick Pritchett to pick her up at her brother's house. Because it was such a showplace, Nick had readily agreed.

The doorbell pealed again just as a deer-trapped-in-the-headlights look sprang up in Rose's blue eyes. Panicked, she looked from one woman to the other. "Oh God, he's here. I'm not ready," she cried, then repeated, "I'm not ready."

"Yes, you are," Erin said firmly, her tone leaving no room for argument.

Her sister-in-law was dressed to perfection in a

hunter-green sheath that not only flattered her figure but her hair as well. The latter had been styled and left casually down rather than up. She really did look good, Erin thought with pride.

"Take a deep breath," Calista counseled. "Slowly. Then let it out. There," she cheered the other woman on when Rose did as she advised. "Do it again and tell yourself you're going to be fine."

"But I'm not," Rose all but wailed.

Calista looked the older woman directly in the eyes as Erin went downstairs to answer the door.

"Yes," she insisted in an authoritative voice, raising it slightly so she could be heard above the fussing noises that Marlie was making, "you are. Now hold it together and go downstairs. Just remember, he's lucky to be going out with you."

Rose looked at her uncertainly. "Come with me?" It was more of a plea than a request.

Calista smiled and nodded. She didn't believe in being a fifth wheel, but in this case it was obvious that Corey's sister needed all the moral support she could get. Funny how things evolved. Growing up with a bunch of brothers had built up her confidence, Calista thought. Obviously it had had the exact opposite kind of an effect on Rose.

After a less than warm greeting from Nick, the couple left for what seemed to be another of Rose's doomed first dates. Once the door was closed, Calista exchanged looks with Erin.

"I don't have a good feeling about this," she confided to Erin.

"Neither do I," Erin admitted. "But I wasn't the one who arranged the date." She frowned, shaking her head as she stared toward the closed door. "I'm going to see if I can get Corey to come up with a list of his single friends. Rose really wants to get married and start a family. She's a sweet woman who deserves to be happy."

"Then she shouldn't be going out with Nick," Calista commented. And then she felt she couldn't ignore Marlie's unhappiness any longer. Within the span of ten minutes, the baby had grown steadily more and more unhappy. Fussing had now turned into wailing. "Speaking of happy, someone definitely isn't," she observed, swaying now to try to soothe the infant. It wasn't getting her anywhere. "I'm going to go change the princess and give her her bottle and hopefully get her to settle down," Calista told Erin. She began to head back toward the stairs. "Maybe I can get her to go to sleep before your brother gets home from his big night out," she said.

"I know he'd really appreciate that," Erin told her. "He loves that little girl more than anything, but I think he's beginning to be a little punchy. She barely lets him get two hours of sleep at a time. "I'm afraid he's going to wind up falling on his face."

And that would really be a crying shame, Calista thought. "I'll see what I can do," she promised, going up the stairs, back to the bedroom that Jake shared with his daughter.

* * *

He'd needed that, Jake thought two hours later as he turned the doorknob in practically slow motion to not wake up his daughter. He adored the little girl, would do anything to keep her, but going out with Corey and just kicking back for a few hours reminded him that he sorely missed being part of an adult world.

At first, when he took custody of Marlie, he thought he'd just continue with his life the way it had been. But adding a baby to his life was not a simple matter of addition. Concessions had to be made. Changes instituted. The advent of eleven extra pounds in his life had turned that same life completely upside down. She'd invaded every single facet, every single inch of his life.

He knew that other people managed to work things out when a baby came along, but that was because there was usually two people working out the logistics. He still needed to figure out how he was going to juggle being a father to a baby and earning a living to provide for that baby.

Any thoughts that Marlie was sound asleep were dashed the moment he walked into the bedroom.

The first thing he saw coming in was Calista, pacing the floor with Marlie in her arms.

"I didn't think you'd still be here." Rose was obviously gone and he'd just assumed that Erin would put Marlie down for the night—or whatever part of the night Marlie intended to stay down.

The batteries that he'd just recharged felt a bit weaker.

Calista noticed that Jake looked a little bewildered and wondered why. After all, he'd left the baby with her.

Why would he think that she'd just up and leave before he returned? Did she strike him as irresponsible? "Erin asked me to babysit, so I figured I'd just wait until you came home."

Something in her tone caught his attention. "Why, is something wrong?" He was tempted to run his hand along his daughter's downy head, but her eyes were shut and she was breathing evenly, which he took as a sign that she was either asleep or almost asleep. In either case, he didn't want to risk rousing her. She needed her sleep and God knew, so did he.

"No, not anymore."

"Not anymore," he repeated uncertainly. That meant that something *had* been wrong. "What was wrong?" he wanted to know.

Calista continued swaying ever so slightly as she talked and answered his question. "You know the way Marlie's been fussing and crying so much?"

He hadn't mentioned that to her, but from the way Calista was talking, he assumed that Erin probably had. "Yes?"

"Well, it turns out that's because she has a really bad case of diaper rash." When she'd arrived to take care of Marlie, the baby had just been changed. There hadn't been any need for her to change the little girl's diaper until she'd taken her upstairs after Rose had left on her date. That was when she'd made her discovery. "When I took off her last diaper, I saw that her bottom was really, really red and she was starting to get a few pockmarks."

Guilt crept in. Was he responsible for that? Had he been doing something wrong? "What can I do?"

"Well, for starters, change her more frequently—check her diaper the moment you suspect it's wet—and that's especially true whenever she makes a 'deposit.'"

Jake's guilt grew tenfold. "I hadn't thought of that," he confessed.

Calista shrugged dismissively, absolving him of direct blame. "No reason you should. You're a first-time dad. Everything about babies is fresh and new for you. Marlie is your learning curve."

He looked at his sleeping daughter, recalling what her little bottom had looked like the last time he'd diapered her this afternoon. It had been an ugly color red. He'd tried to soothe it with medicated baby powder, but had a sinking feeling it wasn't helping. "Do you think I should take her to see a doctor?"

He'd yet to find a pediatrician in Thunder Canyon for his daughter. It was on his to-do list. A list that kept growing longer instead of shorter. Life was getting away from him again, he thought in mounting concern.

"You don't really have to," she told him cheerfully. "I whipped up a salve for you. My mom showed me how years ago. She told me it as something my grandmother came up with. Apply the salve to Marlie's red areas each time you change her and the rash should clear up in about a day or so."

"Just like that?"

"Just like that," she promised, a wide smile on her lips.

He breathed a long sigh of relief. "How do you know so much?"

"Like I said, my mom taught me that. But you start to pick up things as you go along. Don't worry, you will, too," she promised. Calista looked down at the baby in her arms. *Success.* "I think your little princess has finally fallen sleep," she told him in a voice that was only slightly above a whisper.

Turning, she crossed back to the crib that Erin told her Jake had set up just this morning, replacing the portacrib he'd transported with him when he'd driven here with the baby.

Very slowly, she lowered Marlie onto the mattress. She took extra care to leave the infant lying on her back. The night was too warm to cover her with a blanket, so she left it hanging on the railing, just in case.

Pausing a moment to make sure the baby was still asleep, Calista then turned on her heel and made her way over to the changing table.

"This is the salve," she told him, holding up a small plastic container.

He took a tentative sniff. If anything, it smelled like a sugar cookie. Puzzled, he looked at her. "What's it made of?"

"A little bit of this, a little bit of that," she answered evasively, then assured him, "things you can readily find in a pantry." He looked a little skeptical. "The point is that it works."

"And you've already put it on her?" He knew it was

probably a rhetorical question, but he felt bound to ask it.

"Absolutely, the second I saw how red and raw her little bottom was." Calista grinned. "I think I heard her sigh gratefully."

Any lingering doubts he had about leaving his daughter with a stranger evaporated. "I guess Erin knew what she was doing when she told me to hire you as Marlie's babysitter. I feel like an idiot," he confessed. This was completely new territory for him. "I know what to do out in the field. I'm a damn good cop." And he had the citations to prove it. "But I'm a pretty lousy father," he said with a derogatory sigh.

She hadn't meant for him to beat himself up. "The main thing that makes a good father is love and anyone can see just how much you love your daughter. As for everything else, that can be taught," she assured him matter-of-factly. "You give that little girl love and you're going to wind up with a happy kid on your hands."

For a moment, Jake felt as if the young woman before him was the older one, not him, despite the fact that he had about ten, twelve years on her.

Just went to show that you could never tell. That old saying about never judging a book by its cover was never more vividly true than now, he thought.

He had a funny look on his face, Calista noted. Had she made him uncomfortable somehow? Just to be sure she hadn't crossed some line she was unaware of, she asked, "Anything wrong?"

The question roused him out of his thoughts. "No,

everything's fine, thanks to you," he added. He believed in giving people their due. Reaching into his back pocket, he pulled out his wallet. He'd almost forgotten about paying her. "What do I owe you?"

Your undying gratitude and a night out on the town, dancing.

The thought had come out of nowhere, taking her by surprise. She shook it off, grateful that the man wasn't a mind reader.

Out loud she told him, "Erin already took care of that." She'd almost felt bad about accepting the money, but she definitely could use it and practicality won out. "I'll be going now," she added, congratulating herself that she'd managed to leave the note of regret out of her voice. Because if given the chance, she would have liked to have hung around, talking to him. "I really enjoyed taking care of her."

"Even with the fussing?" he asked.

She smiled at that. "Even with the fussing. Give me a call the next time you want to go out—to watch the baby, I mean." That hadn't come out quite the way she'd meant it, but she knew if she continued to correct herself, it would only get worse, so she left it at that. She didn't want Jake getting the wrong idea.

Jake accompanied her out of the bedroom, leaving the door opened so he could hear Marlie cry if she woke up. Mentally, he crossed his fingers that she wouldn't.

"I'll be sure to do that," he told Calista. He touched her shoulder as she turned to go. "And thanks again. I'm really grateful."

Calista kept replaying his words in her head all the way home.

And, if she concentrated very hard, she could still feel his hand on her shoulder.

Chapter Six

Jake had always taken a certain amount of pride in knowing where he was heading, in always operating with at least a general plan in mind for his life.

A sense of order had always helped Jake not only know who he was but also helped him stay on point whenever he was engaged in his work.

But right now, he couldn't help feeling like a playing card that someone had just tossed up in the air along with the rest of the deck. And like that card, he had absolutely no clue as to where or when he would finally land.

He'd wound up taking a leave of absence from the New Orleans Police Department rather than handing in his resignation outright, the way he'd first assumed that he needed to. The leave of absence had come about because when he'd mentioned resigning, Lt. Franco had refused to accept his resignation.

Sympathetic to his predicament—the man was a father of three—the lieutenant had advised him to "wait and see how things turn out." This way, if he decided that he wanted to come back, he could.

The last thing Lt. Franco had told him was that he was holding his position for him "in case things didn't work out." So for now, being here in Thunder Canyon was just temporary, except that the word *temporary* in this case had no defining limits to it. He didn't know if he was going to wind up staying here a month, three, six, a year or forever.

If anything more than a month was involved, he felt as if he needed to get his own place. Erin's house was huge and both she and Corey had insisted that he and Marlie stay here with them, but he still hated to impose like this.

Something to think about later, he told himself.

The real problem was that he had no job to go to, no place he had to be. Erin and Corey had been adamant about having him stay with them so he didn't even need to look into getting an apartment, at least not yet. This all left him completely at loose ends.

He didn't really do loose ends well.

For the umpteenth time, Jake focused on his only present "job," that of being Marlie's father. God knew he was trying to do that to the best of his ability. Even though a part of him was sorely tempted to leave the basics of Marlie's care and feeding to his sister, who clearly doted on the baby, he couldn't allow himself to take that sort of cop-out. He hadn't come here to have his sister take over for him; he'd come here strictly for a little help. For support really, both physical and more important, emotional.

Wow, he couldn't help thinking, what a difference eighteen months made.

Eighteen months ago, he'd agreed to help his partner get pregnant in the most sterile, clinical of ways. Back then, although he clearly got along with Maggie and was attracted to her, his emotions really hadn't been engaged.

Now it was an entirely different story.

A story that had begun even before Marlie had ever been born. As his partner's time drew near, he found himself growing more and more protective of Maggie. A protectiveness that escalated after she'd given birth to Marlie.

"Fat lot of good that did," Jake murmured under his breath as he looked down at his daughter.

Marlie kicked her legs, as if in response to his words. He had his daughter on the changing table, religiously adhering to Calista's instructions about changing the little girl at the first indication that her diaper was no longer fresh.

Despite all his protective inclinations, Maggie had been shot anyway. And he couldn't help feeling that it was his fault. His fault in more ways than one. He hadn't been there for her the way he should have, hadn't been there to cover her back. And the reason he wasn't there was because Maggie had requested to be assigned to another partner.

And the reason for *that* had been because he'd allowed himself to get in too close. To let her see how protective he felt. How much he cared.

In hindsight, maybe he'd been just the slightest bit overbearing, insisting that she wait another three months before going back to work. He should have known how Maggie would react—that she'd do the opposite of what was suggested.

Maggie had informed him that he was stifling her, that he was invading her space and that she thought it would be best for both of them if he backed off entirely. Before he could really protest, she'd gone and requested another partner.

Her new partner had turned out to be a rookie. And Maggie had turned out to be dead three months after she'd gone back into the field.

"If I hadn't wanted to be part of your life so badly, your mom would have still been here," Jake told the little girl, emotions threatening to all but choke off his windpipe. Marlie looked up at him with her wide eyes, as if accepting every word he uttered and not judging him for it. "I'm really sorry, little girl."

"You shouldn't apologize for loving her. You should never apologize for loving someone."

The familiar voice caught him completely by surprise. Swinging around, Jake discovered that he was right. Calista *was* standing in the doorway of his bedroom. Surprise quickly melted into pleasure as it occurred to him that he welcomed her company.

And then he thought of last night. "Am I supposed to be going out again?" If so, no one had mentioned anything to him this time around.

He looked at his watch. It was a little past noon. Corey, along with his brother Dillon, was presently in the in the process of infusing a healthy amount of cash into renovating Grant Clifford's profitable Thunder Canyon ski resort. The hotel had long rivaled the allure of Aspen.

He looked at Calista quizzically, silently underlining his question. She looked too well dressed to be babysitting, but then, she hadn't exactly looked like someone's poor relation yesterday evening.

"No." Calista laughed. On her way out, Erin had opened the door just as she was about to knock. The latter had let her in, then left for a quick errand. "I just stopped by on my lunch break to see how Marlie was doing with her rash." Because the baby was in the midst of having her diaper changed, Calista looked for herself. She was pleased at what she saw. "Looks like I stopped by just at the right time."

Jake was impressed with her sense of responsibility. In his experience, people her age were almost exclusively into themselves and didn't take the time or made the effort to think about anyone else.

"Miraculously, Marlie's rash is almost all cleared up," he told her. "Thanks to you."

"No," she corrected, wanting to give credit where it

was due. "Thanks to my grandmother's wonder salve. Here," Calista said as she began digging through her purse, "I made up a bigger batch for you when I got home. This should tide you over in case she gets another rash. No reason for the little lady to suffer. Ah, here it is," she announced triumphantly.

With that she produced a small plastic jar and handed it to Jake.

Turning it around, he read the side of the medium-size jar. "Moisturizing cream?" he asked, raising his eyes to hers skeptically.

"That was the largest jar I had—other than the mayo jar and that was a little too big. If I put the salve in that, you'd have to scrape the bottom of the jar to get anything."

"Thanks," he said, closing his hand around the jar. He looked at her again. He thought of her comment about this being the largest jar she had. Were the others for skin care as well? What did she need with any of those? From what he could see, Calista Clifton looked like a natural beauty to him. "I don't think you need any kind of 'beauty aids,'" he told her. "You look good just the way you are."

She hadn't expected to feel such an intense inner glow in response to such a simple compliment. After all, he hadn't said that she was drop-dead gorgeous or anything like that. Stripped down, his comment meant that the moisturizer was doing what it was supposed to be doing: keeping her skin moist. Keeping her looking her age. For the first time, she wondered if that was such a good thing.

Another woman might have laughed and said something about preferring to remain the way nature had initially intended her to be, but lying, even the smallest, whitest and most harmless of lies, was not something she was in the habit of doing. So she felt honor-bound to deflect the much-appreciated compliment by telling him, "I look this way *because* of beauty aids."

Jake remained firm in his assessment, not because he was flirting with her—she was a girl and he was a man, for God's sake—but because he liked to think of himself as having a good eye for details.

"All the so-called beauty aids in the world can't make you look beautiful if you're not."

Obviously this man had no experience with a beauty salon, she thought with a grin. And then it hit her. He'd used the word *beautiful*. Did he just mean that in a general, casual way, or was he actually applying it to her, saying that he thought she was beautiful? She wasn't sure, but she certainly wasn't about to ask. What she was going to do was savor the word and pretend he really meant it.

Which meant quitting while she was ahead.

"I'd better be getting back before Mr. Fowler files a missing persons report," she told him.

"Mr. Fowler?" Sealing the tabs on Marlie's diaper, he lifted the little girl up into his arms, then crossed to Calista. The very least he could do was walk her to the front door. "I thought Erin said you were working as an intern for the mayor."

"I am," she confirmed, turning and walking out into the hallway. "But right now, there's only part-time work available for me."

That didn't answer the question entirely. "And Mr. Fowler is—?"

"The owner of that antique shop in the middle of town. You must have seen it, the Tattered Saddle," she supplied the name.

But Jake shook his head as they came to the stairs. "I'm not familiar with it." He hadn't even been aware that there was an antique store in town. He never understood the lure of buying something that was old and falling apart. To him, things like that belonged in the garbage.

"Neither is anyone else, it seems," Calista told him. "I've hardly seen anyone come into the store since I started working there. I really don't know how Mr. Fowler stays open," she confided. "My guess is that he must be independently wealthy, or at least not hurting for money. But then again, he treats every delivery as if it was vital for national security."

Jake stopped walking just short of the upper landing. "I'm afraid you lost me."

"It's like Mr. Fowler has this radar that goes on high alert every time the UPS truck drives up the street by the shop. He gets antsy and starts to act even more peculiar than he normally does. And half the time the truck doesn't even stop at the store When it doesn't, he acts surly and disappointed. When it *does* stop, he practically vibrates like a tuning fork.

"Another thing," she confided. "I was at the front of the store for the last delivery and I offered to sign for it for him so he wouldn't have to go outside. He practically shoved me into the store, telling me to keep dusting. He snapped that it wasn't my 'job' to sign for deliveries. Then he had the delivery man come around to the back of the building and drop the delivery off at the back entrance to the storeroom, otherwise known as his lair."

"His lair?" Jake repeated, amused.

She nodded. The man acted as if it was his private little domain. "He holes up there half the time I'm at the store. Heaven only knows what he's doing in there." She drew upon something she'd been forced to read in English class in her junior year. "Two hundred years ago, I would have said he was Silas Marner, counting his gold," Calista quipped.

It was probably nothing, just an eccentric old man very set in his ways, but nonetheless, Jake could feel the inner policeman in him coming to the fore. It just reinforced his feeling that he didn't do nothing well or for long. What if the old man was up to something? What if the shipments didn't contain antiques but something else?

He was letting his imagination run away with him, Jake thought as he followed Calista down the stairs. This Fowler guy was undoubtedly exactly what he seemed, an offbeat guy with a bunch of quirky habits.

The region seemed to have a crop of eccentric people, he thought.

"Colorful locals" Corey had called them.

Jake addressed the back of Calista's head. "Doesn't sound as if he's a nice boss."

She shrugged. "Not as nice as some," she allowed, glancing back at him over her shoulder, her meaning very clear. "But I can put up with it until Bo wants me working full-time. When he does, I'll leave the Tattered Saddle in a heartbeat."

"Is that what you want?" he asked as they came to the first floor. "A career in politics?"

"In some capacity, yes," she replied. "It doesn't have to be in the front lines, like a congresswoman or a senator," she clarified quickly. Even though she wasn't shy, she didn't have a craving to be in the limelight. "I just want to be involved in doing something that really matters. Something worthwhile. Something that winds up helping people."

He believed her. There was something very honest and sincere about Calista. It was hard for him to believe she was only twenty-two, as Erin had mentioned. "Well, I'd say that you've already gotten a good start doing that kind of thing already, what with the way you've gone out of your way to help Marlie."

Calista stopped just short of the front door and turned around to look at the infant in Jake's arms. As well as to steal a glance at Jake.

"Well, that was my pleasure entirely, wasn't it,

Marlie?" she said, lightly stroking the baby's soft, downy red hair.

In response, Marlie cooed.

Jake laughed, marveling, "I swear she understands everything that's said to her."

Calista smiled. "No reason to believe that she doesn't."

Surprised, Jake raised his eyes to hers. "You believe that?"

The question had just slipped out.

Although he believed to a great extent that babies *did* understand what was said to them, it was ordinarily an opinion he kept to himself because when he voiced it, he was either humored, or just laughed at and asked if he was joking.

"I sure do," Calista replied with genuine feeling. "And I think more and more people do, too. Why else would they tell women to play soft, soothing music for their babies before they're even born?" she challenged. "Seems kind of silly otherwise."

When he came right down to it, Jake had no rebuttal for that. He found himself liking the way Calista agreed with him.

Found himself liking a great deal about this young woman.

And he shouldn't, he reminded himself. She was much too young for him—if he was in the market for some female companionship, which he wasn't. Right now, Marlie was all the female he could handle.

"Thanks for stopping by," he told Calista as she

opened the front door. Belatedly, he realized that along
with his daughter, he was still holding the jar she'd
given him. "And for the extra salve."

Calista waved a dismissive hand. There was no need
to thank her, but she did like hearing the words from
him. "Don't mention it."

"Oh, and about that Fowler guy?" he said just as she
crossed the threshold.

Calista stopped and looked at him, wondering what
he could say about the old man. Did he know him? Was
he going to tell her to ease up on the shop owner?

"Yes?"

"If he does anything else that seems a little off to
you and you want someone to talk to about it, give me
a call."

Did that sound as stilted to her as it did to him? he
wondered. It wasn't a line even if it sounded like one
in hindsight. She'd aroused his curiosity and mercifully given him something to think about other than
his daughter's disappearing diaper rash.

The invitation pleased her, but the last thing she
wanted was to sound too eager. "I don't want to bother
you."

Jake laughed. He would more than welcome the distraction, although, as he'd already told himself, there
was probably nothing to the owner's strange behavior
beyond a quirkiness.

"It's not exactly as if I'm very busy these days. I'm
not doing anything except learning the ropes of being
a father."

"Don't underestimate that," Calista told him. "Some guys never bother learning."

She hoped he didn't think she was talking from direct experience. She was fortunate because her family was close-knit and her parents had been great, but she had friends who'd been raised by single parents, usually their mother, and they hardly saw their father when they were growing up.

Or worse, they had both parents in residence, but one or both were far too self-absorbed to do much beyond provide for the basic physical essentials that went into raising offspring, neglecting them emotionally and thus robbing them of a very important component while they were growing up.

That, she could see, was never going to happen to Marlie. Marlie was going to be one of the lucky ones, she thought, then roused herself. She was getting too distracted again. But then, Jake Castro was a *very* distracting man.

Secretly, she blessed Erin for calling her in.

Her thoughts shifted to Erin.

"When Erin gets back from her errand," Calista told him, lingering a moment longer in the doorway, "tell her I said goodbye."

Calista glanced at her watch again, willing the minute hand to slow down. Her lunch was all but over and she knew that if she was a minute late, Jasper Fowler would have some cryptic comment to shoot her way about not paying her to dawdle and be tardy.

Hell, he'd probably have something biting to say even if she made it back on time.

Waving at Jake, Calista hurried over to the vehicle she'd parked in the spacious driveway and quickly got in. The next moment, the engine hummed to life.

Jake remained where he was, in the doorway. Marlie appeared fascinated with her surroundings and was taking it all in, giving him a moment to watch Calista as she got into her car and then drove away.

He turned what she'd said about the man she worked for over in his mind, wondering if sheer boredom was goading him on, or if there actually was anything to Fowler's behavior.

Calista could have been exaggerating, but somehow, he doubted it. He might be wrong, but she didn't strike him as someone who had a wild imagination she let run away with her.

It did seem rather odd that the shop was surviving while there were, according to Calista, next to no customers frequenting it. Of course, the man could be independently wealthy and running the antique store simply because it was a lark for him.

Jake brightened considerably at the thought of investigating something, however insignificant it might be. He loved Marlie more than he thought possible, but at the same time, being here, away from his job was making him feel as if his police skills were becoming rather rusty.

If he brightened up at the thought of seeing Calista also, well, that was only incidental.

Or so he told himself.

Chapter Seven

The tall, thin man cleaved to the shadows, moving about like a ghost of his former self.

He'd thought—fervently hoped, actually—that this cavernous emptiness that felt as if it was eating him alive would start to recede by now. That at least a tiny bit of the old enthusiasm that had been such an integral part of him would have begun to return.

But it hadn't.

He was empty. A shell. Any ability to feel was still exiled somewhere in limbo, completely out of his reach.

If he felt anything at all, it was guilt. Soul-shredding, gut-wrenching guilt. At times, especially at night, it would descend over him so oppressively that he thought he could scarcely breathe.

Those were the times that he prayed for oblivion, but it didn't come.

Those were also the times when he was tempted to seek his absolution in a bottle, but he knew there were no solutions there, no answers. Using alcohol to blot out his mind only created more problems.

Besides, that was no way to pay Dillon Traub back for his kindness. When his whole world had literally blown up on him and he hadn't known which way to turn, it was Dillon who'd called him, offering him a place to stay, where he could retreat to for as long as he wanted, no demands, no questions.

A place where he could disappear.

He'd taken the lifeline gratefully, and had been living in that mountaintop cabin for more than a month now, venturing out only when he absolutely had to for food and supplies. When he did come out, he said nothing to no one. As far as the people who saw him knew, he was a mute.

A mute who was waiting for the abyss that hovered within him to receded.

Wondering now if it ever would.

The people he moved past in town probably thought he was some deranged hermit. God, would they be surprised to find out who he really was, he thought.

Or more accurately, who he'd been.

After the incident, he didn't know if he would ever be able to go back to his life.

Or even want to.

Carefully depositing the supplies he'd picked up at

the supermarket into the back of the Jeep Dillon had lent him, he felt something hit the back of his calf.

Looking down, he saw that the wind had caught up a flyer from somewhere and sent it traveling. Removing the colorful paper from his calf, he was about to let the flyer continue on its wind-fueled journey when the words *Frontier Days Festival* caught his eye.

Rather than just drop the paper or ball it up to throw away, he paused to scan it. The flyer invited one and all to attend the town's annual celebration. It promised wonderful homemade food, fun rides, friendly competitions for all ages and music by "the best musicians west of Nashville."

For just a split second, the words struck a chord. He stared at them like a man who was completely hypnotized. And then the next moment, he did what he'd initially thought to do. He balled up the flyer, tossing it into the back of the Jeep to be thrown away once he got back to the cabin.

There was no point in thinking about attending the event, not even from the sidelines. If, for some reason, he ventured out to the festival, someone was bound to recognize him there. He had no doubts that in no time at all, the crowd would be in an uproar. Nobody would want him there or anywhere near them.

And he couldn't blame them. Not after what had happened in April....

Resigned, he retreated into the emptiness, embracing it as it encompassed him, blotting out everything else. Rounding the front of the vehicle, he got in on the driver's side and drove back to the empty cabin. To continue repenting the occurrence of something that he hadn't been able to foresee until it happened.

Okay, Cali, for heaven's sake, get a grip!

This was the third time today that Calista had caught her mind wandering, dwelling on the man she was supposed to be helping out. The man she had absolutely no business thinking about.

She couldn't allow herself to go on like this.

It was all well and good to disengage her brain from the rest of her when she was working at the antique shop—how many brain cells did you really need to dust old furniture properly?—but when she was interning at the mayor's office, she was supposed to be sharp, not dull like the stubby point of a kindergartener's worn-out crayon. And she couldn't be sharp if her mind was elsewhere.

Specifically, if her mind was lingering on every single word uttered by the father of the little girl she'd babysat last night.

Babysitting for Jake Castro was becoming more of a regular thing. In the last couple of weeks, her services had been recruited five times since she'd initially agreed to the arrangement. It was at the point that when she went home—or actually, even when she was at one of her other jobs—she caught herself listening for both her own cell phone as well as the landline to ring. Waiting to hear Jake Castro say in that deep, sensual baritone voice of his that he "needed her."

Actually, he hadn't used that particular choice of words, nor had he called to say that he "wanted her" which would have been even better. The word he used was "available." Was she available at such and such a time? But the thought behind the request was there and she had enough of an imagination to fill in the blanks.

So far, the five times she'd been over to take care of his daughter, Jake had gone out with Erin's husband or one of the other Traub men and she'd thought nothing of it.

What if next time he called it was because Jake needed her to watch Marlie because he was going out on a date? A real date with a woman.

The thought and her reaction to it startled her. A shaft of jealousy shot through her like a finely pointed arrow.

Blinking, Calista struggled to pull herself together. At the same time, she realized that one of the mayor's two administrative assistants, Laura Riley, was talking to her—and had been talking to her for at least a couple of minutes now if the look on the woman's face was any indication.

"Are you feeling all right?" Laura asked her pointedly.

Embarrassed at being caught like this, Calista quickly assured her, "Yes, I'm fine."

"Because you look as if you're a million miles away right now." The woman appeared none too happy about the assessment.

No, not a million. More like five miles or so, Calista thought.

But in either case, she shouldn't have been. She wasn't being paid to fantasize about a man, no matter how good-looking he was.

"Actually, I've got a headache."

Mentally Calista crossed her fingers, silently apologizing for resorting to a white lie, something she'd never been guilty of before. But it was just that if the woman thought she was daydreaming or zoning out, it would reflect badly on Bo because he'd been the one who had given the thumbs-up to hire her in the first place. From what she'd heard around the office, Thunder Canyon's new mayor had enough to deal with trying to figure out just what the old mayor had done with the funds that went suddenly missing from the town coffers. There were people who were actually pointing their finger at him rather than the previous mayor, Arthur Swinton, saying that he was somehow responsible for the missing money and that Swinton had been used as a fall guy.

When the fact that the money was missing had initially come to light and Swinton refused to talk, he'd been arrested. The thinking was to leave the ex-mayor in a cell, cooling his heels until such time as he came clean. However, a fatal heart attack had derailed that plan. So at the moment, the sorely needed funds were still missing and the only one who supposedly could tell anyone where they were was dead.

Although she was young and optimistic, Calista wasn't naive. She knew how close-knit towns like

Thunder Canyon worked. Rumors sprang up, fueled by wild speculation. Because of the missing funds, Bo Clifton's base was eroding, not to mention his good name along with it. She couldn't add to that, no matter how insignificantly, by having people in the office think she was coasting exclusively on her connection to Bo.

Laura stood looking at her skeptically. Just as Calista thought the administrative assistant was going to call her on her lie, the woman said, "I've got some aspirin in my desk. I can give you a couple of tablets to get rid of your headache."

Calista smiled her gratitude, taking care to look sincere. An old adage leaped to mind: Oh what a tangled web we weave when first we practice to deceive. She promised herself this was going to be the extent of her fabrication career. Right after this was behind her.

Out loud she said, "That would be very nice of you," surprising herself with the ease with which she could voice and give further life to the white lie she'd created.

This wasn't for her, it was for Bo, she told herself, trying to assuage her conscience. At the same time, she upbraided herself for thinking about Jake.

Laura Riley returned to her rather quickly, carrying a small bottle of water in one hand and presumably two aspirin tablets in the other.

The two small white tablets actually felt warm as Calista accepted them. Then, as Laura continued to watch her carefully, Calista had no choice but to pop the aspirins into her mouth. Taking the bottled water from the older woman, Calista washed down the tablets already decomposing on her tongue.

"Now, whenever you're feeling better—and I trust that'll be soon—I need you to file those reports for me," the assistant declared, leaving a pile of folders on the desk beside her computer monitor.

Again, Calista forced a wide smile to her lips. "The second the aspirin takes effect," she promised, satisfied that at least this time around she'd bent the words so that she wasn't technically lying outright, just being very vague.

Served her right for letting her mind wander like that, she thought, annoyed with herself. The time to think about Jake Castro was when she was somewhere close to his vicinity, not while she was trying to create a good—or at least a decent—impression in the mayor's main office.

After all, this wasn't just about her. She represented not only herself but the rest of her family as well.

With effort, Calista put her thoughts on hold and instead applied herself to the task at hand.

"Calista, would you mind calling me back? I need to talk to you."

She'd been at her desk all morning. She'd finally stepped away for what seemed like a couple of minutes, but obviously, that was when the blinking message on her desk phone had come in. At first, she hadn't even looked at her phone—what were the odds, after all, for her to get a call in that particular limited time frame?

And yet, that was when the call had come through. The persistent blinking light had registered belatedly, negating her brief belief that her mind was playing tricks on her.

The second Calista hit the proper button to play back her messages, she heard a woman's voice. It had taken her less than five seconds to recognize who was calling. Erin. And more than five seconds to tell her accelerating pulse to slow down.

She was going to get to see Jake, she thought, radiantly happy.

You can't be sure of that. Maybe this isn't a call to ask you to babysit. Maybe Erin wants to talk to you about something else.

There was no point in speculating and second-guessing. She needed to call Erin back and find out what was going on before she let her imagination take flight again.

Very carefully, Calista looked around to see if the mayor's administrative assistant was around anywhere. Personal phone calls weren't forbidden, but they weren't exactly encouraged, either. She hadn't seen the woman for the last half hour, which meant that she had either gone to lunch or was in a conference in one of the offices that formed a semicircle around the central work area. In any case, Laura Riley wasn't around at the moment.

Calista took advantage of that and dialed quickly. She didn't have to pause to look up the number. At this point, she knew it by heart.

The phone on the other end of the line rang four times before it was picked up. Calista started talking the second she heard the receiver go up.

"Erin? This is Calista. You called me?"

"Yes." The voice on the other end of the line sounded rather tense and harried. Calista's immediate thoughts gravitated to the baby. Had something happened to Marlie? "Yes, I did. I know this is very short notice, but I was wondering if you were free tonight to come by and watch Marlie?"

She wasn't actually free. One of her sisters had suggested that they all get together tonight and eat out. It was going to be an old-fashioned gab fest. But Erin sounded stressed and she wanted to help if she could. Calista knew that she could get a rain check from her sister. It wasn't as if Colleen would be facing an empty chair if she bowed out. That was the upside of having so many siblings: there was always someone handy to fill the space.

"I think I can rearrange things." Pausing, Calista debated asking a question. She didn't want Erin to think she was invading her privacy, but the other woman did sound pretty upset. Well, there was only one way to find out why.

"Is something wrong?" Calista asked.

There was a long pause on the other end of the line. Calista was just beginning to think she'd offended the other woman when she heard Erin hesitantly say, "It's not my place to say."

Erin remained noble for a moment longer, then

mentally threw up her hands and told her, "Jake got a letter from Marlie's grandparents."

That in itself couldn't be what was upsetting Jake's sister. Calista pushed a little more. "I take it they weren't asking after her health."

"No, they weren't." And now she could hear the anger in Erin's voice. A sister's anger for the wrongs done to her brother. "They were all but accusing Jake of kidnapping Marlie. They said that if he didn't return and bring them their granddaughter, they were going to go to court to sue him for custody."

Calista didn't understand. Unless there was abuse involved, the first people who had custody of a child were the child's parents. Or parent if there was only one available. "But he's the baby's father."

"I know, I know, but it's not that simple."

Calista stopped looking around to see if Laura had emerged and was heading her way. Her attention was now entirely focused on what Erin was saying.

"Oh. Why?"

"Jake said they found a paper in her things. He initially signed it as a formality when he and Maggie first made their agreement. In it, he waived all of his rights to the baby. Her parents are now trying to hold him to it."

That sounded absolutely awful to Calista. She knew that Marlie's grandparents had suffered a terrible tragedy, losing their daughter like that, but getting involved in a tug-of-war with their granddaughter serving as the rope wasn't going to help them come to terms with Maggie's death.

"Marlie's not a car or some property to be handed over from one 'owner' to another," she protested indignantly.

"You don't have to sell me on that," Erin told her. "You're preaching to the choir. Look, Corey has access to this team of corporate lawyers because of the oil company. I thought that maybe Jake could talk to one of them, get a handle on what he can do to somehow make this all go away. One of the lawyers said he could come by and talk to him. I want to make sure that there aren't any distractions for Jake. So could you come and watch Marlie for him?"

Put that way, even if she was inclined to go out with her sisters, she wouldn't have turned Erin down. "Sure. What time do you want me there?"

"Mr. Coen said he could be by at seven. So how about six-thirty?" Erin asked, knowing that anything earlier would be difficult for the other woman.

"That sounds fine to me," Calista told her. "See you then."

Terminating the call, she took out her cell to call her sister and see about rescheduling dinner.

Jake looked angry when he opened the door to let her in. He was holding Marlie in his arms. "Hi, thanks for coming on such short notice."

"Don't mention it." She looked at the baby. She could have sworn there was recognition in Marlie's eyes. "Hi, sugar, how're you doing?" She took the baby from Jake with practiced ease. Holding Marlie on her hip, she looked at the infant's father. "Anything I can do to help?"

"You're doing it," he pointed out. "Corey's bringing one of his lawyers over to talk to me."

"Those are corporate lawyers," she told him. "Don't you need to see a family lawyer?"

"Down the line, yeah, but Corey's already called this guy and he's knowledgeable enough to help me plan a strategy. Corey said that this lawyer—Coen, I think he said his name was—can give me a referral."

She nodded, taking in the information. Calista felt awful about what he had to be going through. "They can't just take her away from you," she said with feeling. She wanted him to know that she was on his side. "You're her father. You have rights."

Nervous, he began pacing the room. He'd feel infinitely better once this was finally resolved and he could get on with his life with his daughter. "And they have this piece of paper that I signed, giving up those rights."

She had taken a number of classes in law to help her in her chosen field. Calista did her best to recall what she'd learned. "You can say you signed that paper to give Maggie peace of mind. Under those conditions— her raising your baby—you didn't want her being afraid that you'd come after custody one day. But everything's changed," she reminded him. "Now that she's gone, your bargain with her is null and void."

He looked at her skeptically. That sounded almost too good to be true. "Can I do that?"

Marlie had grabbed a fistful of her hair and was trying to pull it out. Tears came into Calista's eyes as she worked to gently take her hair out of the tightly closed little fist. For a baby who wasn't even a year old yet, Marlie was almost freakishly strong.

"With the right lawyer you can," Calista managed to tell him without crying out in pain. "More important, with the right judge. Anyone can see that you love this little girl," she told him, swaying with Marlie to keep the baby from protesting the loss of the strand of hair she'd been yanking. "You put your entire life on hold and came all the way out here just to make sure that she has everything she needs. If that's not demonstrating how sincere you are, not to mention how stable, I don't know what would."

He knew the judge would be looking at the bottom line as well as the total picture. Mr. and Mrs. O'Shea had money and, married for thirty-five years, they represented a stable family unit. He had a family to fall back on, but that wasn't the same thing as a wife and he knew it. "Maggie's parents have the resources to give her a good life."

Calista shook her head. There were more important things than money. "She belongs with her father. You love her."

He felt a sense of desperation for a moment, a desire to just grab Marlie and flee. "I know it and you know it, but the law's not always fair."

"What would convince the court that you can provide Marlie with a stable home life?"

He shrugged. "If I was married, they'd probably look at me differently," he answered. He'd actually asked Maggie to marry him; that was when she'd gone ahead and asked for another partner. Jake laughed shortly. "I'm not even in a relationship. How am I supposed to find someone to marry me?"

Calista looked from the baby to him and without hesitation said, "You could ask me."

Chapter Eight

Jake stared at her, stunned. The woman his daughter took to so readily couldn't possibly have meant what he thought she'd just said.

"Ask you what?" he asked her, enunciating each words slowly.

"Ask me to marry you. Because I would," she told him. He looked so stunned that she quickly added, "So that you could keep your daughter. We'd be married strictly on paper." She further explained so he didn't think that she was trying to use his situation to trap him in a marriage for some secret reasons of her own.

While the idea of marrying Jake had more than a little appeal—so far she hadn't found a single thing about the man that she didn't like, or was even merely neutral about; from where she stood, the man was the

total package—Calista didn't want what she'd just offered to scare him off.

And while she might daydream about what life might
be like if she were married to Jake—or someone like
him—she really didn't want to get married for at least
a few years. But he was apparently in a real bind and
if this meant that he could keep his daughter, she was
confident that they could come up with some kind of
an arrangement that would be satisfactory to both of
them.

The sound of crockery disastrously meeting tile momentarily brought the conversation—such as it was—to
a skidding halt. They both turned toward the doorway,
where the sound had come from, to see what had happened.

Erin was standing just inside the living room, an utterly stunned expression on her face. She'd been walking into the room, carrying a tray of beverages and
homemade cookies when she'd overheard Calista tell
Jake that she'd marry him. Momentarily dazed, she'd
forgotten all about the tray she was holding. It tilted,
sending everything on it to the floor in a shower of cups
and cookies.

Just what was going on here? Erin wanted to know.
She looked from her brother to the girl she'd opened her
heart up to. Was Calista serious? When had this devel-
opment occurred?

Frozen in place, Erin continued to stare at Calista.
"You didn't just say—?"

Erin didn't get a chance to finish forming her

question. Second-guessing what she thought the other woman was going to ask, hurrying over to gather up the scattered baked goods and cups, Calista spared her the awkwardness as she cut in and said, "Yes, I did. I said I'd marry Jake so that he could keep Marlie."

She was actually serious, Jake realized. This wasn't a joke.

What kind of a person offered to make that sort of a sacrifice? It wasn't as if Calista was an old family friend or even a personal friend he'd had for a while. Granted the woman was warm and outgoing and there was something really inviting about her, not to mention attractive, but that was just the point. A woman like that could have her pick of men and marriage would undoubtedly be in her future if she wanted it. Not only that, but it would be on her terms. She definitely didn't strike him as being one of those women who was obsessed with getting married by a certain age.

That made this a selfless act on her part. Of course he couldn't accept, but in light of what had just been said, he looked at the woman with fresh insight.

"I appreciate the offer," he told Calista with feeling, "but I don't think I'll really need to resort to doing that."

Finished gathering together the items that had fallen and placing them back on the tray, Calista rose to her feet and nodded.

"Hopefully, your grandma and grandpa will be reasonable about this, little one," she said, addressing the words to the baby.

In the distance, they could hear the front door being opened.

Erin instantly brightened. "Corey's back," she announced.

That was her cue to leave, Calista thought. She took the baby from Jake. "Marlie and I'll get out of your way," she told him.

With that, she made her way to the stairs.

Jake glanced after her as Calista and his daughter left the room. She wasn't just the attractive, exceedingly capable babysitter anymore. She was now someone who was willing to put herself out more than he had the right to ask, just to help in the fight to keep his daughter if it came down to that. He marveled once more at the kind of person she was and he couldn't help being impressed by her—again.

Heartened, he went to meet with the lawyer Corey had brought home with him.

Reaching the second floor, Calista paused for a moment, thinking. Rather than go to the bedroom Jake shared with his daughter, she debated giving in to her curiosity.

Curiosity won.

Calista positioned herself just a little shy of the landing to listen without being observed. From her present position, she couldn't be readily seen by the people who were now in the living room discussing Marlie's future and what courses of action were open for Jake.

They couldn't see her, but she could easily hear them.

She remained there for a few minutes. Sleepy, Marlie cooperated by dozing off and on in her arms, affording her the perfect opportunity to eavesdrop.

Part of her couldn't believe she'd just said what she had to Jake. The words had just tumbled out almost of their own volition. She hadn't known she was going to make the offer until she was actually making it.

And now that it was on the table, she was oddly calm about it. She had no desire to withdraw it or say something flippant to get herself out of it, like she had no idea what she was thinking when she said that.

That, undoubtedly would be what her siblings would say, though, if this marriage of convenience should actually become a necessity. They'd want to know what the hell she'd been thinking and quite honestly, she couldn't answer that question. All she knew was that once the words were out, she had no regrets, no panicky feeling in the pit of her stomach.

On the contrary, she felt like smiling. Nervously, maybe, but still smiling.

"Would you like that, sweetheart?" she whispered to the sleeping angel in her arms. "Would you like me to be your mama?"

Marlie went on sleeping.

Funny, although she'd been involved in taking care of her younger brothers and sisters—and at times coming through for her older ones as well, giving her the feeling that she was *everyone's* caretaker—she hadn't really thought about the prospect of having children of her own. That, if it actually was to transpire, was something that she'd felt was still years and years away.

But that feeling suddenly changed today as she listened to the sadness in Jake's voice when he talked about losing his daughter. He'd tried to cover it—she had the impression that he didn't like letting anyone see that he actually *could* be vulnerable—but she'd detected it anyway. And she didn't want him being sad, didn't want him losing his daughter and she definitely didn't want Marlie to become a pawn in a custody battle.

She had no doubt that his late partner's parents were grieving and that their pain over losing their daughter was genuine. But forcing Jake to give up his wasn't going to make anything right.

And while she sympathized with them, her real sympathies, not to mention her loyalties, lay with Jake.

So much so that she was willing to assume the title of his wife for Jake to retain custody of his daughter.

"Who would have ever 'thunk' it, huh, little one?" she whispered again, this time saying the words softly against Marlie's downy head. "A month ago, I didn't even know you existed, and here I am, volunteering to be your mom."

A month ago, she hadn't known that *Jake* existed, she thought. And here she was, saying she'd be his wife. Not *pose* as his wife, but go the whole nine yards with a marriage license, ceremony and everything.

Well, at least the whole eight yards, she silently amended. The marriage wouldn't go beyond being one on paper. She knew she could trust him to be a gentleman and not try to consummate the marriage.

The corners of her mouth curved ever so slightly.

That really wouldn't be so bad either, she mused. If he went beyond the confines of a marriage on paper. If this marriage was a marriage not just in name only, but in all possible ways.

Calista closed her eyes for a moment, letting her imagination take off.

She'd be willing to bet that Jake was a very good, caring lover. Not that she was all that experienced, but she just had a feeling....

You are definitely getting too carried away here, she told herself.

From the bits and pieces she was picking up from the conversation downstairs and the advice Corey's lawyer friend was giving him, Jake wasn't going to need a wife on paper or otherwise, at least not in the immediate future. Possibly never.

A sliver of disappointment pushed itself through, momentarily stinging her before Calista blotted it out. Okay, at least she wasn't going to be faced with an incredible amount of explaining to do and her siblings weren't going to marvel at how impetuous she could be if put to the test, she thought. There was an upside to everything, however minor.

Marlie began to stir in her arms. She didn't want to risk having the baby's noises reach the people downstairs. It would take very little for them to connect the dots and realize that she'd been eavesdropping on them.

Even though she had, she didn't like the kind of image that it presented.

"Let's go see about entertaining you," she told Marlie as she retreated from the landing.

It was almost another hour before Jake came upstairs and into his bedroom, looking for her. He found her sitting in the rocking chair that Erin had bought for him. She was slowly rocking Marlie as she fed the baby her bottle.

When she saw him coming in, Calista immediately snapped to attention, trying to gauge whether his mood was optimistic or resigned by looking at his expression. Maybe it was her imagination, but he seemed to be a little less tense, which she took to be a good sign.

"How did it go?" she wanted to know. Calista deliberately kept her voice low so as not to disturb the baby.

For his part, Jake was cautiously optimistic, afraid to become too hopeful. But even more afraid to entertain the alternative thought.

"It went well, I thought," he told her. And then he sighed, as if to release the breath he'd been holding for the last few hours. As he spoke, he embraced the hope his words embodied. He was determined not to lose Marlie no matter what, but it would be a great deal easier on both of them if the path was not complex and stressful, or involve fleeing and hiding.

"Turns out that Corey's friend used to be part of a family law practice before he decided to go into corporate law. He's going to take on the case for me and thinks we stand a pretty good chance of resolving this early." He grinned for the first time as he added, "Without your making the ultimate sacrifice and marrying me."

"That wouldn't be the ultimate sacrifice," she corrected matter-of-factly. Then her mouth curved as she added, "Giving you both my kidneys, now that would be the ultimate sacrifice."

He laughed shortly at the exaggeration. "Lucky for me, I don't even need one."

"Lucky," she echoed.

Glancing down, she saw that Marlie had emptied her bottle. She set it aside and shifted the infant, placing Marlie against her shoulder. With small, rhythmic strokes, she began to pat the baby's back, waiting for the obligatory burp to emerge.

For a moment, Jake debated saying anything. Debated asking. But his sense of curiosity finally prompted him to voice his question out loud.

Sitting down on the bed and facing her, he asked, "Why did you do that?"

She felt the baby close her little hand on the shoulder of her blouse and clutch it. The contact spread a warm feeling through her. Without meaning to, she had bonded with Jake's baby. Very strong feelings came along with that bonding. Maybe that had motivated her to make the offer she had. It certainly hadn't prevented her from volunteering.

"Well, if you don't burp her, that could leave some trapped gas inside that tiny tummy and more than likely, it'll make her really uncomfortable." She smiled at him. "And you already know that if baby isn't happy, *nobody's* happy. She'd be up all night crying."

He shook his head. "I'm not talking about burping her," he told Calista. His eyes held hers. "I'm asking why you offered to marry me."

Calista looked away. "I told you, to keep you from losing Marlie."

There had to be something more. Was she *really* just that altruistic? "I know the reason behind the gesture. I want to know why *you* personally made the offer. I don't know anyone else—women I've known a lot longer than you—who would have done that for me."

She shrugged, not wanting him to make a big deal of it. Most of all, she didn't want him overthinking the offer and reading into it. It wasn't as if she expected him to behave like a *real* husband.

"I don't think it's right for them to take your daughter from you and if that's the only way to help keep you from losing her, I would have felt guilty knowing that I could have stepped up and didn't." She laughed softly. Marrying him for the sake of the baby wouldn't complicate her life all that much. "It's not as if I'm in a committed relationship and have to worry about breaking the news to my boyfriend."

It was the first time that he caught himself wondering about Calista as a woman rather than just an exceedingly friendly, helpful person. Were there men in her life? A relationship that she was hoping would turn into something special?

"Are you in an 'uncommitted' relationship?" Jake asked.

"I'm not in any kind of a relationship—right now," she qualified.

She didn't want him thinking that no one found her attractive enough to linger with and have him wonder if possibly *that* was the reason she'd made the offer in the first place, so that she could tell the world that at least *someone* wanted to marry her.

Her answer hadn't mattered—until she gave him the right one. Why else was there this sense of relief flowing through him? And why was there suddenly this strong pull toward her within him? Was it entirely based on gratitude, or was he really seeing her for possibly the first time?

He was definitely experiencing a feeling of relief, Jake admitted to himself. Relief that there was no competition to butt up against.

But that was ridiculous.

Calista was in a completely different decade than he was. She was a whole twelve years younger. Twelve years difference when you're ninety meant nothing. But at this point, it did, he silently insisted. For Calista, life was just beginning, promising a whole spectrum of adventures, of sensations she'd yet to experience, while he'd already had some of those adventures and was now thinking that settling down wouldn't be such a bad idea. He told himself that he was ready for a different stage of life than Calista was, a far less exciting, more stable one.

Marlie burped. Calista smiled and patted the little

back one last time. "Good job," she told the baby cheerfully.

She just offered to marry you, how much more stable than that can you get? he silently demanded.

"Good thing," he heard himself murmuring as Calista rose to her feet. She raised a quizzical eyebrow, asking for an explanation, before she crossed to the crib and placed Marlie down on her back. "Because if you were in any kind of a relationship," he explained, "there might be some guy out there looking to clean my clock for stealing his girl."

"Don't worry," she told him. "If there was such a guy, which there's not," she underscored, "I wouldn't let him 'clean your clock.'" She couldn't help smiling at the strange expression he'd just used, even as she echoed it. The words were a tad old-fashioned. She wouldn't have thought it of him just by looking at the man.

He looked, she thought, like trouble. The kind of trouble most women prayed all their lives to run into, at least fleetingly. A "bad boy" who was two steps away from being converted to a good guy.

There she went again, letting her mind wander and take flight. She had to stop having fantasies about this man. There was no point and it would only wind up leading to frustration.

Turning from the crib, she found herself accidentally brushing up against Jake. The unexpected contact sent strong currents of electricity coursing through her veins. They turned out to be so strong that they all but took her breath away.

Startled, her eyes widened as she looked at him.

Dealing with his own rather intense response to the split-second brushing of body against body, Jake took a step back.

"I'm sorry," he apologized, not wanting her to think he'd stood there in her way specifically so that this could happen.

Her eyes locked with his. She was going to say something casual and dismissive like "That's okay," or "No harm done." How the words "I'm not" emerged from her lips instead, riding on a sultry whisper, she had absolutely no idea.

The next moment, an all-encompassing wave of embarrassment washed over her. It would have completely obliterated her if it had had the chance. But as it turned out, it was pushed to the background by what occurred next.

Time seemed to literally stand still as Jake cupped her chin in his hand.

Then, leaning in, he brushed his lips against hers and kissed her.

And very effectively, set fire to her little world as she knew it.

Chapter Nine

Calista melted. Quickly.

A moment before she would have attained the chemical composition of a bowl of soft ice cream, she slipped her arms around Jake's neck, leaning into his, seeking strength.

Seeking sustenance.

Seeking heat.

Because she could feel it all radiating from him, drawing her in, offering her shelter.

Her head was spinning madly.

Meanwhile, wild, wonderful things were happening all through her. She hadn't exactly been living under a rock for the last twenty-two years but she might as well have been, she thought. Because nothing she'd ever experienced before could compare to this. It was as if she'd been taken apart, molecule by molecule, and then entirely rebuilt.

Thrilled, eager, delighted, with her last measure of strength Calista deepened the kiss, letting him know as best she could that if this was some sort of a happy accident, a momentary slip on his part, that he hadn't offended her or taken advantage of her. She wanted him to know that she enjoyed being kissed by him. Moreover, that she didn't want this to be the last time that he did kiss her.

Wow.

The single word lit up in large, powerful neon lights inside his head. All Jake could think was that for such a little thing, Calista packed one hell of a wallop. It had certainly knocked him for a loop. Who would have thought that beneath that sweet exterior something akin to a tigress existed?

Amid the swirling storm of emotions and the impact of her kiss, common sense burrowed mightily up to the surface. Intent on holding him accountable.

What the hell was he doing? his common sense demanded as he struggled to do his level best to extricate himself from the jaws of unadulterated pleasure.

The answer to the question was that he didn't know. He'd just meant to quickly brush his lips against hers, to thank her and let her know that he appreciated her earlier offer and that he thought that she'd been genuinely generous to make it.

He'd had absolutely no intentions of getting lost in her kiss, or even to kiss her like this, with every single emotion he possessed suddenly rising to the surface and jumping into the fray. He certainly hadn't intended to knock his socks off in the process.

She was hardly more than a kid, he silently insisted. How could he be having these feelings about her?

The answer, he told himself, was simple. He *wasn't* having these feelings. What was happening was simply a rebound reaction. He'd been in love with Maggie and she had closed herself off from him and then she'd died, leaving him with all these feelings, all this love, all of it unresolved.

Forcing him to take them all elsewhere.

But he wasn't really *feeling* what he thought he was feeling. It was all just an illusion, a trick of the mind. A distraction engineered by his psyche to allow all those hurt feelings he was carrying around to heal.

He didn't feel things for this bright-eyed woman with the silver laugh. Wasn't reacting to her. Wasn't feeling that strong pull inside him toward her. He just *thought* he was.

But first, he told himself, he had to stop kissing her because it was fogging up his mind.

With effort, Jake took hold of her hands and removed them from around his neck. Then, their lips still sealed to one another, he put his hands on her shoulders and pushed her back gently, driving the all-important wedge between them and ushering in light, space and air.

Calista blinked, realizing that her lungs were seriously depleted of oxygen. She drew in a breath as unobtrusively as she could.

At least she wasn't panting, she congratulated herself.

Looking at Jake, she thought she saw regret flash in his eyes. Was that regret that he'd kissed her, or regret that he'd stopped?

She knew which side she was voting for.

"You're not going to say you're sorry again, are you?" she asked, bracing herself for the worst, hoping for the best.

Had he recovered more quickly, the apology would have already been out there. But she clearly didn't want to hear him say that, Jake could tell by the apprehensive expression on her face. He was lucky she'd taken his breath away like that, otherwise he would have said he was sorry and that, he could see, would have insulted her. She definitely wasn't acting as if he'd forced himself on her, so that was a relief.

"Wasn't planning on it," he replied, instincts now telling him what she'd want to hear. It was a relief to be honest.

"Good," she told him with an approving nod. "Because I would have hated to have to punch you out after we'd just shared something so special."

The second the words were out, she realized that she was being too honest for her own good. But then again, that was a flaw of hers. She'd never gotten good at those mind games people her age were supposed to engage in. She didn't believe in them and most likely, she probably wouldn't be any good at them even if she subscribed to playing those kinds of games.

"I didn't mean to embarrass you," she added on after

a beat. "My sisters are always telling me that I have a tendency to be too honest. They say that it gets annoying."

"I'm not annoyed," he told her. "And honest is good." His tone said he gave the trait very high marks. "That way, there's no confusion, no wondering if I've offended you and you're just being nice."

"I'm always nice," she was quick to tell him. Amusement danced in her eyes. "And you *didn't* offend me," she assured him. "As a matter of fact, I'm so far from offended, if I were a train, I'd be stationed in the next county."

It took him a second to wrap his head around the metaphor. That had to be a first, a woman comparing herself to a train. Charmed, Jake laughed, shaking his head. "Calista, I have a feeling that you're one of a kind."

"I'd ask you if that was good or bad, but I think I'd better quit while I'm ahead."

"Good," he told her. Then, in case she misunderstood, he elaborated further. "It's good."

Jake glanced at his watch. It wasn't even nine o'clock yet. He no longer needed Calista's services tonight and the best thing right now would be just to send her home so that she could salvage some of the evening for herself, but he found himself really loathe to have her leave just yet. He liked her company, liked talking to her.

He searched for a way to detain her a little while. And then his stomach growled. He went with that. "Did you have dinner before you came?"

She shook her head. There hadn't been time. "I came straight here from the mayor's office." While she liked to cook for her siblings, the idea of cooking just for herself aroused no pleasure. Takeout was a good way to go. "I'll just pick up something on my way home," she told him.

Corey and Erin had left for the movies the moment the lawyer had driven away. That left them alone in a house that was large enough to house a full three-ring circus with room to spare. He didn't want to be in the house alone just yet.

"If you want to stick around for a while," he proposed, "I can make us something to eat. It's the least I can do."

She was surprised by the offer. "You cook?" He didn't seem like the type who ventured into the kitchen for any other reason than to get a beer.

He didn't want her expecting miracles. "I did use the word *least,*" he reminded her. "But yeah, I do cook. Not well," he admitted, then quickly added, "but passionately."

His usual method was to start out with a recipe, then just take off creatively. However, in this case, he figured he should rein himself in a little when it came to the seasonings he added. A lot of people didn't like hot, spicy food the way he did.

Calista definitely liked the way he said that. "Passion is good."

He looked at her for a long moment. Coming from

her, the word took on a whole different meaning. "Yeah," he agreed quietly, "it is."

A warm shiver danced up and down her spine. For a second, she almost gave in to impulse and kissed him, but she stopped herself at the last moment.

This was by no means over, she promised herself.

"C'mon, let's go downstairs," Jake urged.

She murmured, "Okay," as she fell into step beside him.

As he crossed to the doorway, Jake paused a moment to pick up one of the receivers that went with the baby monitor.

"It's a big house," he explained as he eased the bedroom door closed behind them. "I might not hear Marlie when she cries and because there's no one else home right now who might be able to hear her cry and alert me, having the monitor on is the next best thing." He raised a quizzical brow as he looked at her. "You don't mind, do you?"

"Mind?" she repeated. How could he possibly think that she'd mind his being a responsible parent? He just went up ten more points in her book, bringing him to an almost-perfect score. "I think it's wonderful. And I think that Marlie's grandparents are absolutely crazy to try to take her away from a father who's as caring as you are."

He shrugged away the compliment. Words of praise, whether in the form of a commendation at work or something more personal in nature on the private front, always embarrassed him. He never knew how to respond and he'd never been one for the limelight.

He deflected the compliment by saying, "I've got a lot of faults."

Well, it was obvious that a swelled head wasn't among them, Calista thought. "Last time I looked, that was part of being human."

"Definitely using you for a character witness if the O'Sheas decide to drag me into court," he told her as he walked down the stairs behind her.

She fervently prayed that it wouldn't come to that for him. But if it did, she was going to convince him that her earlier offer definitely still stood.

He'd intended to cook while she took it easy. It didn't turn out that way.

Less than three minutes into the project, he discovered that, like him, Calista didn't do sitting on the sidelines very well. He'd barely begun to put together his own version of a Spanish omelet, gathering eggs, potatoes, onions and a small, lethal jalapeño pepper when Calista got off the stool and began plucking additional ingredients out of the pantry and the refrigerator.

Not only that, but somehow amid all this she also managed to clean the bowls, wire whisks and measuring utensils practically at the same time they were being pressed into use.

When Jake was finished creating his spicy masterpiece and the end result was neatly divided between two dinner plates, waiting for her verdict as well as for consumption, he looked around the kitchen and marveled at its immaculate state. Everything was washed and dried and back in its place.

The woman was a magician, he thought.

Or a witch.

A very sexy, enticing witch.

"You know, usually when I cook it looks as if a hurricane had come through, following me around," he confided. The description had come from Maggie, who had been on the receiving end of his culinary efforts several times. He glanced around again, still awed by how swiftly this slip of a thing could work and move. Calista was nothing if not full of surprises. "This doesn't even look as if I was here." He laughed. "I think Erin's seriously going to consider adopting you."

"I'm a little too old for that," she answered, amused. "But I don't do sitting on my hands, idle, well," she told him. "I like to pitch in and help." She couldn't remember a time when she didn't.

"You're holding down two jobs and helping me out by watching Marlie. As far as I can see, you don't have any idle time. Which reminds me." He put his plate down on the counter and dug into his back pocket. Taking out his wallet, he flipped it open. "I haven't paid you for tonight yet." So saying, he took out several tens. But before he could give them to her, Calista pushed his hand back. He looked from the money to her, puzzled. "Not enough?"

"Too much," she countered. Before he could ask how that was possible, she went on to say, "Tonight's on the house. I really wasn't here long enough to charge you any money."

She was wrong, he thought. On purpose? But why? "By my calculation, you were here watching Marlie for more than two hours. You're still here," he added with an amused grin.

"Not exactly babysitting right now, am I? Chalk it up to one friend helping out another," she told him. *A friend who managed to curl another friend's toes. How can I take your money after you did that?* "Besides," she said out loud, "you're feeding me."

She hadn't tasted the end product yet. "According to my sister, you might want to charge *me* extra after you taste my efforts."

Now he was just being super-modest, she thought. "If it's that bad, you wouldn't have offered to cook dinner in the first place," she pointed out.

He laughed. She had him there, he supposed. "You're pretty sharp."

"For what?" Calista pressed. His tone indicated that there was more to the phrase than that, a part he'd left unsaid. "For a girl?" she supplied, then suggested, "For an intern?"

Why would she think that he would insult her by saying that? "I was going to say you were pretty sharp for someone so young."

He made it sound as if she was in kindergarten. "Not so young," she corrected. "And you're not exactly approaching social security anytime soon, you know."

Then, in case Erin hadn't mentioned it, she told him her age. "Jake, I'm twenty-two."

He already knew that and it was what kept eating at him. He found the age difference between them a huge chasm. It only made him feel guiltier about these budding feelings that refused to be pushed aside or shut away. "Exactly, and I'm thirty-four."

Her eyes widened as if she'd been utterly knocked off her feet. "And you're not using a walker? Isn't that taking a huge risk? Does your caretaker know what a daredevil you are?"

"I didn't realize that you were such a wise guy," he told her.

She looked at him for a long, pregnant moment, letting it draw out before telling him, "There are a lot of things about me you probably didn't realize." A Mona Lisa kind of smile graced her lips. She indicated the two plates resting on the counter beside the baby monitor. "Now, let's eat before your creation starts to get cold," she urged.

"Good point."

Sitting down beside her at the extended bar facing the other side of the work island, Jake watched her beneath hooded eyes as she took her first bite.

He waited to see her reaction, wondering if her eyes were going to water or if he'd be able to detect a trace of a telltale frown fleetingly creasing her lips.

There was neither.

Instead, the first bite was followed by another, and then another. Her eyes rose to his and she pronounced the effort "Very good." And then she looked at him suspiciously. "Why aren't you having any? Should I worry that you sprinkled oleander powder on the omelet when I wasn't looking?"

She'd read somewhere that, odorless and tasteless, the flowering plant was nonetheless very poisonous. It could be ground up and added to food with the intended victim being none the wiser.

"Really one of a kind," Jake murmured, repeating what he'd said earlier.

In response to her deadpanned question, he took a bite from his own plate, then reached over to hers and took another bite-size piece from her plate.

"There," he said once his mouth was empty again, "that should prove that both portions are safe," he told her. "I was just watching to see your reaction to the omelet. I didn't want you just being polite while meanwhile, you felt as if your mouth was on fire."

"My mouth *was* on fire," Calista contradicted, a secretive smile curving the corners of her mouth as she looked at him. "But trust me, the omelet had very little to do with it."

Her words drew a warm smile up to his lips before Jake was even aware that his mouth was smiling. Despite his best efforts to hold her at bay, she was having a definite effect on him.

"So you like the omelet," he finally said.

"Very much. Personally, I think the bits of ham, bacon and especially that green pepper really make the meal." It was a teasing remark. The ingredients she'd mentioned, all finely diced and chopped, were her personal addition to the mixture.

Jake looked up from his plate, his eyes meeting hers. There wasn't even a hint of a smile on his lips as he said, "I think so, too."

Warm ripples of pleasure undulated all through her. She didn't remember eating the rest of her portion. What she did remember, quite vividly, was the man who was sitting beside her, and the effect he was having on her while she ate.

Chapter Ten

Jake looked at himself in the bathroom mirror. He'd never been a vain man, and right now, he felt as if he looked like hell. But there was a reason for that.

He hadn't slept, at least not long enough for his body to recharge.

The night had been one long tossing-and-turning fest, rendering him unable to sleep for more than approximately two hours at a time, at which point he'd wake up and begin the struggle to get back to sleep all over again. It had turned out to be a losing battle.

For the first time since he'd become a hands-on father, his sleep-deprived night wasn't because Marlie's crying was keeping him up. Wonder of wonders, his daughter had actually slept through most of the night and he hoped it was a sign of things to come—just as he hoped his restless night wasn't.

Dressed and shaved, he went downstairs, hoping that breakfast might make him feel half-human.

Part of the reason he hadn't been able to sleep, he knew, was because he was sincerely worried that he was going to have to resort to drastic measures to keep from losing custody of his daughter.

But part of it had nothing to do with Marlie at all except, perhaps, in the most cursory sort of way—if he hadn't had Marlie, most likely his path would have never crossed Calista's.

Hell, except for having come to Thunder Canyon for Erin and Corey's wedding, he wouldn't even have been here at all if not for Marlie. He'd still be a cop back in New Orleans and in all likelihood, both he and Calista would have lived out their lives without ever even having a conversation, much less one as serious as the one that they'd had last night.

Before Calista had gone home, she had restated, rather forcefully, that she'd meant what she said: if he needed her to become his wife to keep his child, she was willing to do it.

By that point she'd convinced him that she'd made the offer in all sincerity and he, God help him, was actually considering it—and not just because it would allow him to keep Marlie. He'd begun to entertain the thought because he was more than just a little attracted to the vibrant, enthusiastic young woman.

They were as different as night and day. She was

dawn to his dusk. She was lively while he was stoic. And yet there was…*something*. Something there that drew him in, that attracted him to her.

And the fact that he was so attracted to her bothered the hell out of him. He was a responsible person, a cop, a father, and he should know better than to have these sorts of feelings about a recently graduated *college student,* for heaven's sake.

Didn't that make him a cradle robber or something along those lines? He was too old for her, too old to be having these kind of thoughts about her.…

And yet…

And yet she made him feel good. She made him laugh and feel alive.

He stood at the landing for a minute and dragged his hand through his hair. Damn, but he wished he was still working so he didn't have all this time to do nothing else but just think. In his case, thinking wasn't highly recommended.

He didn't realize that he'd sighed loudly until he walked into the kitchen and Erin turned around from the stove and looked at him.

"Bad night?" she asked sympathetically.

He frowned, thinking of the handful of semi-formed dreams he'd had all centered around Calista last night, dreams that startled him enough to make him jerk awake, then left him to lie there, staring off into the dark and feeling guilty.

"Yeah."

Erin thought for a moment. "I didn't hear Marlie crying during the night."

Opening the refrigerator, he stared into it. Now that he was down here, he didn't know what he wanted to eat. Ambivalence had invaded every nook and cranny of his life. "That's because she slept through most of it," he answered absently.

Erin didn't understand. "Then what kept you up?"

He finally closed the refrigerator, coming away empty-handed. "Other things."

And then Erin understood—or thought she did. "You're worried about losing her, aren't you?" She wanted to throw her arms around him, to hug him, but she knew that wouldn't really help. "Oh, Jake, don't worry, we'll fight this." She knew Corey was more than willing to help and heaven knew he had the resources. Jake didn't like being indebted to anyone, even family, but these were special circumstances. "We won't let those people take Marlie away from you."

Looking around, Erin suddenly realized that there was something missing. She remembered leaving pots piled up on the drying rack, not to mention dishes in the dishwasher. A quick check told her that the dishwasher was now empty, as was the drying rack.

Her eyes shifted back to Jake. "Did you clean the kitchen last night?" she asked with more than a hint of disbelief in her voice. Jake wasn't a slob, but he never cleaned up after anyone else.

"Calista did." He opened the refrigerator again. This time, he took out a carton of orange juice. His stomach was growling. "She cleaned up while we were making dinner."

Erin backed up mentally. She knew Jake knew how to warm things up in a microwave, but this sounded a lot more serious than that. "You *cooked* for her?"

Taking down a glass from the cupboard, he set it on the counter and filled it with juice. "It was more of a combined effort." He paused to drain half the glass. "I started to make her dinner to thank her for her offer and she wound up pitching in." His eyes met Erin's as he went on to marvel, "And everything that was used, she washed a second after we were finished using it. Never saw anything quite like it."

Something in his voice caught Erin's attention. He sounded intrigued, for lack of a better word. Did Jake have feelings for Calista?

"You're not really thinking of marrying her, are you?" she asked, feeling him out. "I mean, I know these kinds of things are done, but they're done by other people. Not people like us, like you," she insisted. "There should only be one real reason to get married, because you love each other." Her expression grew very serious. "Don't get me wrong, she's a great girl, but you and Calista hardly know each other."

He'd never liked being lectured to, however softly put and well-intended. It got his back up. "You and Corey didn't exactly grow up together," he pointed out.

From what he recalled, Erin had been working as a receptionist at the new, rebuilt Thunder Canyon Lodge when she met Corey, who'd been brought in along with

Dillon as a major investor in the new resort. When they'd gotten married it was at the end of what was a fairly whirlwind courtship.

Erin forgot about breakfast. What her brother was alluding to was far more interesting. "Are you saying you actually have feelings for Calista?"

Jake shrugged, not so much looking away from Erin as looking into his soul. Searching for answers. Could what he was experiencing be called "feelings"? Or was he just being vulnerable, a word—and concept—that he loathed to apply to himself?

Except that it was true.

"I'm saying there's chemistry and if that's a way to keep Marlie without turning this whole thing into some three-ring circus, or dragging it endlessly through the courts, well, maybe I shouldn't just turn my back on it without exploring the possibility more fully." He saw the set of his sister's mouth and laughed shortly. "I thought I was the stoic one in the family. What happened to the devil-may-care sister I had?" he wanted to know. "The one who used to say that tomorrow would take care of itself and that she just wanted to live in the moment? The one who said never let an opportunity go by without grabbing it and using it to your advantage?"

"She got married and grew up, not entirely in that order," Erin answered. Reaching up, she put her hand on her brother's shoulder and said with deep sincerity, "I just want you to be happy, Jake. And I definitely don't want you to do something because you have to instead of because you want to."

"I'll be happy if I can hang on to Marlie," he said evasively, avoiding making a direct response on how he felt about Calista.

"It'll work out," she promised him.

"I know. One way or the other," he added. Then, before she could say anything further about the situation, he asked, "Now, any chance that I can get you to whip me up some breakfast? I'd do it myself, but you're a much better cook."

She laughed, brushing her lips against his cheek. "You smooth talked me into it. Go ahead, take a seat."

Opening up the refrigerator, she began taking things out to prepare a large breakfast for all of them.

"Are you out of your mind?"

Lingering over a superlight cup of bracing hot coffee, Calista looked up as her older sister, Catherine, came into the kitchen. So much for grabbing a few peaceful minutes alone with her coffee before heading off to work, she thought.

"Not that I know of," Calista responded with studied cheerfulness. "Are you referring to anything specific, or is that just a general philosophical question?"

Slightly taller than her younger sibling, Catherine Clifton had the same willowy frame, the same long brown hair and the same deep chocolate eyes.

And right now, they weren't smiling, and neither was she.

"Erin Traub called me last night, said you offered to marry her brother, Jake, so that he could get to keep his baby daughter," she retorted, then demanded angrily, "What the hell were you thinking?"

"My guess is fringe benefits," Celeste, the sixteen-year-old baby of the family, better known to one and all as C.C., said as she walked in on the tail end of the conversation.

Still wearing pajamas despite the fact that it was eight in the morning, C.C. went to the coffeemaker and poured herself a cup of black liquid. Calista, she thought, always knew just how to brew an excellent cup of coffee.

"Lighten up, Catherine," C.C. urged. "Have you *seen* Jake Castro? Talk about your mouth-wateringly delicious male…" Her voice trailed off as she grinned wickedly. "Listen, Cali, if you change your mind about marrying that hunk, tell him I'm willing to jump in and take your place."

"You're sixteen, you can't jump in anywhere without parental consent," Catherine informed her coolly. She thought of their mother, a very loving woman who indulged her children only so far and no more. "Good luck with that."

"Mom and Dad raised us to make sacrifices for good causes," C.C. pointed out with a wicked gleam in her eyes. She loved baiting her older siblings, all except Calista who she thought was very cool. Besides, Calista always took her side in things. In her book, loyalty was rewarded with loyalty.

"And my sacrifice will be to lock you up in your room until you're thirty," Catherine fired back.

C.C. frowned as she looked at Catherine over her coffee mug. That didn't make any sense. "How is that a sacrifice for you?"

That was simple enough. "I'll have to listen to you screaming night and day."

Calista cleared her throat. And then cleared it again when no one seemed to hear her the first time. "Excuse me, people, but I can't see why something I 'might' be doing is anybody's business but my own." She might have said it as if she was talking to both of her sisters, but she was actually addressing Catherine.

Catherine looked at her as if she couldn't believe that her sister had to ask. "We're family. Everything you do is our business," she answered matter-of-factly. "Haven't you learned that by now?"

C.C. looked at Calista and begged plaintively, "Take me with you when you go. *Please.*"

"Nobody's going anywhere yet," Calista told C.C. How had her simple offer snowballed like this? "Marrying me is just Jake's last resort."

Catherine rolled her eyes. "How very romantic," she quipped drily.

"This isn't about 'romantic,'" Calista insisted. "It's about saving a baby from being dragged out of her father's arms by two people who seem to think they know best."

Talk about the pot calling the kettle black. Catherine gave her sister a penetrating look. "And you have no idea what that's like."

Calista hadn't expected her sister to exactly cheer

her on, but she had expected a little more support from her than this. To find out she was wrong both hurt and annoyed her.

"Why are you on their side?"

"Wrong again," Catherine declared. She placed a hand on Calista's shoulder. "I'm on *your* side. Always." There was compassion in Catherine's eyes as she said, "I just don't want you making any mistakes, kid."

If it came down to that, and she did marry Jake, she realized that Catherine was afraid Jake might take advantage of that fact.

"Don't worry. We'd only be married on paper," Calista assured her. "It would all be platonic."

"Hello?" C.C. called out, pretending to knock on Calista's head. "Again, have you *seen* Jake Castro? Who in their right mind would want to stay platonic with someone who looks like *that?*" she wanted to know.

Catherine was studying Calista again and drawing her own conclusions. Beneath the supposed noble act was a woman with feelings. Feelings for Erin's brother. "Not our sister, I'm willing to bet."

"Hey, I'm already on record about my feelings—" C.C. reminded Catherine.

"Not you, that sister," Catherine corrected as she nodded at Calista.

Even when they were children, Catherine had always had this annoying habit of being able to practically read their minds, so protesting was not the way to go. Calista tried another route.

"I'm not saying I don't find him cute—" she began with a half-careless shrug.

"Cute?" C.C. echoed incredulously. "When was your last eye exam? Kittens are cute," she pronounced dismissively. "That man is drop-dead-and-rise-up-again-from-the-grave gorgeous. How can you not want to jump his bones the first chance you get?"

"I am *definitely* locking you in your room," Catherine declared with a frazzled sigh as she poured herself a second cup of coffee.

C.C. raised her chin, as if to issue a dare. "Do your worst," she challenged.

"And while I'm at it," Catherine continued, "I'll chop down that big tree outside your window."

"Now you're not playing fair," C.C. protested with a pout.

"I'm older and wiser. I don't have to play fair," Catherine told her.

"Well, I hate to bring an end to this lovely family bickering," Calista announced as she rose to her feet. "But I promised Mr. Fowler that I'd come in for a few hours today to help him put out the new furniture he got at the Mayfield estate auction last week." She crossed to the sink and quickly rinsed out her cup, then deposited it on the rack.

C.C. shook her head. "Don't know how you can stand to be around all that ugly furniture." Extracting a bottled banana smoothie out of the refrigerator, she proceeded to retreat back into her room.

"No breakfast?" Catherine asked Calista as the latter turned to head out the front door.

"No time," Calista answered, then added, "I used up all my extra time defending myself." The words were said matter-of-factly, without a hint of accusation.

Still, Catherine pressed her lips together as she followed her younger sister out. "It's just because I love you."

Calista grinned. "I know."

Doubling back to grab a bagel—plain, no butter— she quickly hurried out the door.

When she heard the front door to The Tattered Saddle being opened several hours later, Calista glanced up from her boring task, grateful for the break in tedium, even though it probably wouldn't result in anything.

Saturday was when people who worked all week indulged in window shopping and browsing in stores. However, a place like the Tattered Saddle rarely attracted customers. Those who did come in were generally forty-five or older, able to relate a little better to the merchandise that was being sold or, more accurately, resold, because most of the pieces there had had at least one previous owner before finding their way into the antique store.

Calista did a double take, the identity of the customers—or rather customer and a half—registering a beat after she initially looked up. She was prepared to see one of her sisters, most likely C.C., or even one or more of her brothers—word spread fast in her family. She was *not* prepared to see Jake come walking in, with Marlie nestled in the carryall he had hooked over his forearm.

Abandoning the feather duster she'd been waving about for the last hour in the losing battle with dust, Calista swiftly made her way over to him.

After directing a fleeting smile at the baby, she shifted her eyes to Jake.

"Is something wrong?" she asked him, concerned. Was this it? Had he come here to tell her that he had to take her up on her offer?

Butterflies began to rev up in her stomach as they filed a flight plan.

He could feel the charged energy radiating from Calista. Something in her eyes spoke to him. Stirred him. He had to watch that, he warned himself.

Age difference. Think of the age difference.

"No. Marlie and I were just making a formula run," he told her. Which was true, as far as it went. "And she wanted to see what you did when you weren't changing her diaper."

Glancing over her shoulder to see if Fowler was coming out of the storeroom—he wasn't—Calista still lowered her voice as she told him—and Marlie, "My other job is a lot more interesting. And a lot less dusty," she added. At the mayor's office, she had a desk and the office just had a more important feel about it.

She realized she wanted to impress him and that just wasn't going to happen in the antique shop.

If he was being honest with himself, Jake had to admit that curiosity was partially to blame for his impromptu visit. The things Calista had told him about Fowler the other day, that the old man seemed so jumpy whenever he was waiting for a delivery, that she had no idea how he kept the business going when no one showed up, all that spoke to the cop in him. The cop who had had nothing to do in the last month and was going to go stir-crazy if he didn't get to use his investigating skills very soon.

Looking around, Jake saw nothing really out of the ordinary. Nor did he see any customers. He also didn't see anything in the furniture that was on display that moved him. In his opinion, what he saw was a collection of depressing furniture. He could see someone selling it just to be rid of it. What he couldn't see was anyone paying good money to buy it.

"And there's actually a market for this?" he asked, making no attempt to hide his surprise.

Calista glanced around, taking in the whole lot as she shrugged. "So they tell me. Like I said, I have no idea how he hasn't gone bankrupt. If Fowler sells one piece a week, he's going good." She glanced at her watch. Impulse caused her to say, "You know, I'm almost done for the day. Why don't you wait here and I'll just tell him I'm leaving."

In all likelihood, it would probably make no difference to Fowler whether she told him she was leaving or not. But she had a certain sense of responsibility and that wouldn't allow her to just slip away. There were rules of decorum to follow, even if the old man wasn't the type to appreciate that.

Crossing to the back, Calista knocked on the door leading into the storeroom. Receiving no answer, she tried knocking again.

When she'd knocked a third time without getting a response, she tried the doorknob. To her surprise, it gave. Fowler always locked his door. Had he forgotten, or was there something more to it than that?

She wasn't going to find out just standing here, staring at the door.

Holding her breath, she began to turn the doorknob.

"What the hell do you think you're doing?" Fowler snapped out the question as he came up behind her, entering from the side of the building.

Startled, Calista swung around. "You weren't answering when I knocked. I thought there might be something wrong."

Her concern about him made no impression. It was as if he hadn't even heard that part, or possibly was too cynical to believe it.

"What's wrong," he informed her, his voice growing louder with each word he spoke, "is that you're a little snoop looking for an excuse to go into the storeroom when I expressly told you not to go in."

"You have no cause to talk to her like that," Jake said, restrained anger in his voice as he stepped up to defend Calista.

Turning around, Fowler did a quick assessment as he swallowed his initial retort. The man doing the talking was a lot bigger than him. Stronger-looking, too.

"You're that cop from New Orleans, aren't you?" It

was an assumption, voiced out loud, rather than a question. "Well, this isn't New Orleans, so you can't order me around."

"Not ordering, just telling," Jake said. "She was just trying to find you to let you know she was leaving for the day."

"Okay, you've let me know," Fowler told her. "Now leave. And take your cop friend and his kid with you," he ordered, waving her away.

With that he turned his back on all of them and strode into the storeroom. He slammed the door shut in his wake.

"You heard the man," Calista said. She couldn't wait to put this place and its incredibly rude owner behind her. "Let's go."

Struggling to contain her anger, Calista led the way out.

Chapter Eleven

"I'm sorry about that," Calista apologized once they were outside the store on the sidewalk. It wasn't often that she actually got angry, but when she did it was like trying to contain a raging forest fire. It wasn't something that she achieved easily. "Fowler has no right to behave that way toward you."

But Jake brushed aside her apology. "I'm the one who should be apologizing to you," he told Calista. Turning back, he looked at the store behind her. "I didn't get you in any kind of trouble, did I?"

"Not the kind that would matter to me," she retorted, her anger aimed at the scrawny, angular man who was back in his storeroom, doing who knew what. "Like I said, this job's only temporary until I start really working in the mayor's office on a full-time, full-salaried basis."

Which she could only pray would be soon. Right now, the office was filled with summer interns, but come fall, they would all be returning to their respective colleges, and she would still be here. With any luck, a permanent position would open up for her then.

"But in the meantime, you need that job to help with expenses," Jake surmised, nodding toward the store.

She shrugged carelessly as she tossed her head to underscore how little that mattered to her. She deliberately kept her back to the store and began to walk toward her car.

"I'll manage," she assured him. "Trust me, I know how to cut back."

She'd done it before and besides, her needs were modest. She wasn't one of those women who needed to go on a shopping spree every time her spirits needed lifting. For one thing, she was usually incredibly upbeat.

She was just saying that to absolve him of blame, Jake thought. It wasn't working, but her effort once again showed him the kind of solid, good person she was.

"You shouldn't have to," he countered. Moving in front of Calista, he held out the carryall to her. "Here, hold on to Marlie, I'm going to go in and have a few words with Fowler, make this all right."

Rather than take the carryall, Calista raised her hands up as if she was going through the motions of surrendering. However, surrendering had nothing to do with it. She was counting on the fact that if he had to hold on to his daughter, he wouldn't go inside and confront the eccentric shop owner.

"No, please, really. Like I told you, he's just a quirky, weird old man. You'll be wasting your time and your breath trying to reason with him. To be honest, I don't think he does enough business to even warrant having a part-time sales clerk. All I do for the most part is dust for him. Besides, I don't want to see you getting worked up on my account. At least not this way." Her eyes widened as, belatedly, she realized what she'd just let slip. "Did I just say that out loud?" she asked him, horrified. A splotch of pink was already beginning to climb up her cheeks.

The remark had surprised him, but he recovered quickly. The least he could do was save her from embarrassment. So Jake looked at her innocently. "Say what?"

He said it so convincingly that she thought for a second that she *hadn't* really said the incriminating words out loud, that she'd only thought them in her head the way she'd meant to. But then she saw a fleeting glimmer in his eyes, making her realize that he was only feigning ignorance for her benefit.

It made her feel closer to him. Her initial impression of the man was dead-on. He was good and decent. He wasn't taking advantage of her slip of the tongue. Or teasing her about the direction her thoughts were running, which would have mortified her.

She knew enough to quit while she was ahead. For now, she retreated with a semblance of her dignity still intact.

That they would get together eventually—and soon—she had no doubts. It was just something she could feel in her bones, but she wanted to be able to pick her own time and place, or at least set the stage and let *him* think he picked it.

And so she shook her head, taking the lifeline he'd thrown her. "Nothing. Never mind."

"Okay." He turned and indicated where his vehicle was parked: down the block and across the street. If she wasn't busy, he wanted her to follow him back to Erin's. "The only right thing for me to do in this case is to take up the slack."

She wasn't sure exactly what he meant by that. "And that would be by doing what, exactly?"

"Having you over to babysit more often," he answered. To him that was the only right thing to do. If he wound up costing her that half-baked job, he was ready to step up and do the right thing. Besides, it would give him an excuse—and a chance—to see her more often which in itself was something he found quite desirable.

She knew his heart was in the right place, but... "I can't just come over to babysit for no reason," she protested.

"Oh, but you'd have a reason," he corrected. "You'd be over because I asked you to come over to watch the baby. And you can't say you don't have the time because you do."

If Fowler let her go, which she had a feeling he probably would, then yes, Jake was right. She would have the extra time. She was only at the mayor's office three days a week and one of those days was only half a day. Calista caught her lower lip between her teeth. Jake was really tempting her—for more reasons than simply the extra money.

But her conscience forced her to make one more protest. "Really, you don't have to do this."

"Are you saying you don't want to babysit?" he asked, moving the carryall in front of him so that Calista could see Marlie better.

Marlie had a face and a disposition that would melt the heart of a rock. Now, as she cooed, was no exception. "No, of course not. It's not that. I just don't want you to feel guilty—"

"I don't," he interjected quickly, shooting down her first protest.

"Or obligated."

He shook his head. "Never crossed my mind," he lied. "You're good with her and she enjoys your company." *Just like her father does,* he admitted silently. "So I just thought that if that old guy decides to cut back your hours or lets you go altogether," he added, saying what was on both their minds, "I can really use your help at least part of that time, if not more. What do you say?"

She knew Jake wasn't exactly rolling in money. He

was a policeman. A policeman on leave—who knew how much of a salary, if any, he was drawing? She refused to tie him down to any sort of promise of the future. "What I say is that we take it one day at a time."

She was certainly behaving more maturely than a lot of other people he knew, he thought. Anyone else would have either jumped at the chance to earn more money or, at the very least, utilized the guilt he was obviously wrestling with and turned it to their advantage.

This one, on the other hand, behaved as if she was wise beyond her years. He liked that.

You're just trying to give yourself permission to do what you really want to do with her and it isn't having her babysit, a small, annoying and exceedingly pragmatic voice in his head mocked him.

Refusing to continue to torment himself, Jake blocked the voice and locked it away. Instead, what he did was bask in the sound of Marlie giggling with something that sounded exceedingly close to glee as Calista entertained the baby by making a funny face at her and then tickling her.

There was no doubt about it, he thought, watching. His daughter was crazy about Calista.

That, he finally admitted, *makes two of us, Marlie.*

"You sure you'll be all right?" Erin asked Jake for the third or fourth time.

Concern burned brightly in her blue eyes. She and Corey were going away for a quick weekend in San Francisco.

When her husband had first mentioned the impromptu trip to her last night, it had sounded both wonderful and exciting to her. But her eagerness to get away with Corey was marred by her concern over abandoning Jake and his daughter, leaving her brother to fend for himself after she'd specifically invited him to come stay with them so that she could help him out with Marlie. It just seemed hypocritical to her somehow. She wasn't going to be able to enjoy the trip if guilt was part of the baggage she was packing and bringing alone with her.

"I really hate leaving you alone like this, Jake. If you'd rather I stayed behind, I will," she volunteered. "I don't have to go with Corey."

Jake could just see how *that* would go over with his new brother-in-law. He lightly took hold of his sister by the shoulders and held her in place to make her listen and see reason.

"Yes, you do," he insisted. "I don't want my brother-in-law to think you're bailing on him because you've got a helpless brother who doesn't know which end is up. Besides, I'm not helpless," he insisted. "Erin, I'm a cop, remember? I'm trained to know what to do in case of an emergency."

"Right, an emergency," she echoed. "Like in a hostage situation, which is great if someone decides to take the house hostage, but you've never trained to be a dad—" she tried to point out, but he cut her off.

"But I'm learning all the time," he reminded her. "I'm getting a lot of on-the-job training. Besides," he continued with a touch of pride, "I think I've been doing very well." He'd been parenting now for close to six weeks, four of those weeks under Calista's watchful eye when he could get her. "And if I need help, I can always call on Calista," he pointed out.

That had been the second thing she'd done after she learned about the proposed trip. The first had been to thank Corey. Properly.

"Speaking of which, I already did. Put her on alert," she added in case Jake didn't understand her meaning. "I called Calista and told her we'd be away. I asked her to look in on you while I was gone, see if you needed anything."

What I really need isn't anything that would be found in a babysitting manual.

The thought raced across his mind despite the complacent expression he was consciously maintaining on his face for his sister's benefit.

Erin paused significantly, her eyes all but penetrating right through him. If he didn't know better, he would have sworn at that moment that she'd transformed into a mind reader.

But then, he decided that it was just his own conscience bothering him, making him paranoid. On the bright side, that seemed to be happening less and less each day, he noted happily. That might be due to the fact that these days he was seeing Calista in a different light than thinking of her as just some barely beyond-her-teens babysitter. After the incident with Fowler, she seemed to him to be far more together than the women he'd gone out with who were far older than she was.

She was, he'd decided, in a class by herself. A class he knew he wanted to have access to.

A few more words on his part and he congratulated himself that he had won Erin over. At least he didn't have to feel guilty about being the reason she canceled out on Corey.

Corey and Erin left bright and early the next morning, heading down to San Francisco for three days and two nights.

Because they had no live-in servants, that left him alone in the large house with his thoughts and his daughter. Jake decided to put the former on hold as he immersed himself in playing and caring for the latter.

The perfect plan lasted for only a few hours, then began to fall apart.

Marlie began to be less and less interested in playing or being entertained. None of the funny faces he was making were working. He began to grow concerned as his daughter vacillated between being listless and being progressively more cranky and distressed.

When she pushed aside her bottle and started to cry pitifully, he was more than just mystified. He was worried.

Picking up Marlie to comfort her, something else registered.

"Is it me, or are you warm?" he asked.

Marlie answered by upping the volume of her cries. Again.

His mother, Jake recalled, would always kiss his

forehead when she wanted to see if he had a fever. His father used to tease her about her "mother's temperature taker," but now, in lieu of a thermometer—something he *hadn't* thought to pack up and take with him—Jake found himself doing the same thing. He brushed his lips against Marlie's forehead. And grew more concerned.

"You *are* warm," he declared, dismayed.

Marlie's response was to wail louder, even as she tried to shove her fist into her mouth, something he'd always taken to be an indication that she was hungry. Except that she wasn't. She didn't seem to want to have anything to do with her bottle when he tried to give it to her again.

Dismay turned into really deep concern.

Confused, wondering if he should just put her into her car seat and drive over to the emergency room, Jake didn't hear the doorbell the first time it rang. Only when it rang a second time, much longer this time—it sounded as if someone was physically *leaning* on the bell—did the noise in the background register with his brain.

With effort, he tried to organize his brain and focus—what *was* it about this pint-size human being that could make him unravel so quickly?

"I'll be right back," he told Marlie, momentarily leaving her in the portacrib he'd set up in the living room. Marlie continued wailing.

Striding toward the front door in giant steps, Jake threw it open. His initial intent was to send whoever was on the other side away, after he got them to stop leaning on his doorbell.

"What the hell—"

He got no further.

The rest of the chastising words died on his tongue before being spoken. In place of the hot words came cool relief. The cavalry had mysteriously arrived on his doorstep without even being summoned.

"Calista!"

On the way over, she'd felt a little self-conscious about coming here after her shift at the mayor's office had ended. She'd actually debated turning back and just going home instead at least twice. Granted that before leaving this morning, Erin had called and asked her to look in on Jake and the baby, but since that incident with Fowler—who hadn't fired her after all—Jake had taken to calling and having her come over, either to watch the baby or just help out with her. That meant that he wasn't self-conscious about asking for her help. If she just showed up like this, he might start thinking of her as being too pushy. That in turn, she thought, could lose her all the ground she'd earned in the last couple of weeks.

But while she didn't want to take a chance on that happening, some kind of inner instincts, a gut feeling, had made her overlook all that and show up on Jake's doorstep anyway.

She just hoped she was right.

The moment he opened the door, her concern about appearing pushy evaporated. The look on his face—and the plaintive cries coming from inside the house—told her she'd made the right call in coming here.

She didn't even get the chance to tell Jake that Erin sent her, asking her to look in on him. Calista barely opened her mouth before he grabbed her by the wrist and pulled her into the house.

"I think she's sick," he cried without a single word of preamble or greeting. There was a thread of fear running through each word he uttered.

"Is she throwing up?" was Calista's first question as she followed him into the house.

Aware that he was squeezing it too hard, Jake let go of her wrist.

"No, but she doesn't want to eat and she hasn't been herself all day. At first she was just listless, but now she's cranky and crying. And she's hot," he concluded, his voice growing loud at his final pronouncement.

Calista smiled to herself. At less than a year old, the casual childless observer would have said that a baby didn't yet have enough of a personality to allow someone to saying that she wasn't "acting like herself." But Jake no longer belonged to that class. He was neither childless nor a casual observer, not anymore. He was now talking like a father, like a *real* father. Despite his concerns to the contrary, and his initial feelings of inadequacy, he'd made the transition nicely.

"What else did you observe?" she asked him as they walked into the living room.

His eyes swept over Marlie in the crib, then shifted

over to her, but only for a moment. Marlie owned all his attention. "She's been crying a lot. More than usual."

Calista heard a lot in his voice. She heard the helplessness he was feeling, plus the frustration. Dealing with him in the last month, she'd come to learn that Jake Castro was a fixer. He liked to make things right and this was something beyond his scope to fix. Just as Maggie's death had been something that was beyond his scope to fix.

Feeling frustrated like this just reinforced his sense of helplessness, which also fed on his exasperation. It was a vicious cycle.

"And she's hot," he repeated as she bent over the crib to pick up Marlie.

Calista made her own quick assessment.

"Warm," she corrected, using the same method to check Marlie's temperature as he had. She brushed her lips against the baby's forehead. *Definitely warm, not hot,* she thought again. Then, holding the baby, she looked at him expectantly. "What else?" she pressed again.

He stared at her, confused. What was she fishing for? Why weren't they getting into his car and going to the hospital?

"What do you mean, 'what else'? Isn't that enough?" he demanded, then said the obvious. "She's not supposed to be running a fever."

For now she decided to spare him the little talk about how children up to the age of about seven were prone to running fevers, sometimes twice in one day, having it go up, then down, then up again and quite possibly down again, too. All mercifully without damage. Usually.

He didn't need that kind of information now. She, on the other hand, did need information. Information he hadn't given her yet and that he possibly didn't even know he had, if it existed.

"You're a policeman, Jake. Think like one." It was more of an order than a coaxing request. "What else did you notice about Marlie today? Or possibly last night? Think," she repeated.

He didn't know what she was fishing for, which only fueled his exasperation, making it grow. "What else is there?" he demanded.

She thought of the baby's age. And the toothless grin she usually sported. She hadn't wanted to put words into Jake's mouth, but there seemed to be no other way. "Has she been drooling?"

He shrugged. "She always drools," he said. "She's a baby. She's messy."

There was messy, and then there was *messy.* "More than usual?"

He scowled as he thought, trying to remember. He supposed it had seemed a little excessive to him now that he thought about it. "You could say that. Why?"

Calista didn't answer his question. Instead, she fired off another one of her own. "Has Marlie been shoving her fist into her mouth even when she's not hungry?"

Again, he stopped to think for a second. "Yeah,

okay, she's done that," he conceded. Concern trumped frustration. "What's it mean?"

Instead of answering, Calista turned on her heel and made her way into the kitchen, still carrying Marlie in her arms. Jake followed in her wake, firing questions at her that went unanswered.

"Here, hold her for a minute," she requested when they reached the sink.

As he watched, not knowing what to make of any of this, Calista washed her hands. "What are you going to do?" he wanted to know.

"Put her over your shoulder," she instructed. Standing on her toes—he was a tall man, she couldn't help thinking—she proceeded to put one finger into the baby's mouth and felt around.

"What are you doing?" he demanded again, this time with more authority.

Finding what she wanted, Calista grinned and withdrew her finger. She had her answer for him.

"Congratulations, Office Castro. You are no longer the father of a toothless baby. Your little girl is growing up." She smiled up into what was possibly the handsomest baffled face she'd ever seen. "Marlie is cutting her first tooth."

That was impossible. "She's too young for teeth," he protested.

"Apparently not," she contradicted. "Mine, my mother told me, started coming in when I was four months old. She claimed it went along with the fact that I was born talking."

A tooth? All this fuss over a tooth? Then why was Marlie running a fever? Was that typical? "So I don't have to take her to the emergency room?" he asked uneasily.

"Only if you have your heart set on a long drive and a longer wait." The look in her eyes went a long way toward reassuring him. "She'll be fine, Jake, really. All babies go through this. It's not pleasant for them—or us—but they do survive. In the meantime, give her something cold to suck on. It'll help ease the pain." He still looked lost, so she gave him a suggestion. "Does she have any teething rings?"

He thought of all the things he'd found in Maggie's apartment that she'd bought for the baby. He'd just thrown everything into boxes and taped them up when he'd moved here, thinking he could sort everything out later. He was still sorting.

"I think I saw one in one of the boxes," he recalled.

It beat sending him into town to the supermarket. "Go hunt it up for me. Meanwhile I'll see if I can distract our princess until you find it."

He nodded, hurrying away.

He was probably too distracted to realize she'd slipped and referred to Marlie as "our" princess, Calista thought.

She crossed her fingers and fervently hoped she was right.

Chapter Twelve

"You really look worn out," Calista observed when she dropped onto the sofa beside Jake some two and a half hours later. Marlie had finally, *finally* settled down and fallen asleep, hopefully for at least a few precious hours. "A little like you've been wrestling alligators all day."

"I kind of feel that way, too," Jake confessed. He felt completely drained as he took in a deep breath and then let it out again.

He did sound as if he'd been through the wringer at least twice over, she thought, as her heart went out to him. "Well, there's good news. I think Marlie's finally dropped off to sleep."

"If she did, it's all thanks to you," he said gratefully. "You did the lion's share of walking the floor with her."

He couldn't help wondering where she got all that energy from. Right now, he'd give anything to be able to tap into it as well. As it was, he was struggling to try to pull himself together. If he didn't, he was liable to fall asleep on her in mid-sentence. "What you are," he informed her, "is a godsend."

She allowed herself to savor the compliment for a split second before shrugging it off. "I don't know about that. I'm more of an Erin-send." When Jake shifted in his seat to look at her quizzically, she explained, "Erin called to tell me that she and Corey were going out of town for the weekend and she asked me to please look in on you after work, whether or not you called." Which did bring a question to mind. Sitting up, she turned to face him squarely. "Why *didn't* you call?" He'd clearly been distressed about Marlie when she'd appeared on the doorstep.

He'd thought about calling her. More than once. But he could be stubborn when he wanted to be and he wanted to try to handle this himself. After all, Marlie *was* his daughter, which made her his responsibility, not Calista's.

"I didn't want to keep bothering you."

In light of the fact that they did have a business arrangement of sorts, that really didn't make any sense to her. "You pay me every time I come over to watch her. How could asking me to come by to look in on Marlie possibly 'bother' me?"

"You do have a life," he pointed out. "If you have to

keep running over every time I need you, you won't be able to live it."

Didn't he understand that by coming over to help take care of Marlie she *was* living her life? That this was something she was good at and enjoyed doing? Not to mention that more than half the time, he was around for the duration as well. Being here allowed her to talk to him and enjoy his company under the pretext of baby-sitting his daughter.

"Taking care of that little girl *is* part of my life," she told him. Then, for good measure, she added, "My life is what I choose it to be, and I choose to help you out with Marlie. I *choose* to be around that little person to do what I can so that things go a little bit more smoothly for both of you." She looked at him pointedly, trying to make him see that she wasn't some lightweight who could be easily overwhelmed and didn't possess a backbone to speak of. "Next time, if you need me, pick up the damn phone and call. If I can't come, I'll tell you I can't come. Don't try to second-guess me."

"You've never told me that you couldn't come," he reminded her. And he didn't know if that was because she was actually free or if she was afraid of turning him down when he called.

"Because," she said simply, "so far, that hasn't come up."

And she doubted that it ever would, but she wasn't about to tell him that. Instincts told her that not everything needed to be spelled out at this point. Especially not because their relationship, such as it was, was still fresh and not quite formed.

She was acutely conscious of the fact that Jake hadn't kissed her since that one isolated time. So what did it all boil down to? Had the kiss been a fluke? A miscalculated accident on his part? Had he absolutely no desire to revisit the scene of the crime to see if perhaps it could get better?

She really didn't know what to think. There were times, like now, when she felt she was getting certain vibes from him, but that could be just a reflection of her wishful thinking, her own unanswered needs.

She just didn't know.

Meanwhile, Jake was busy, thinking and carrying on a silent argument with himself. Frowning, he looked up at her. "You think Marlie might be upset because I moved her out?"

The question had come at her out of the blue. It took Calista a couple of seconds to connect the dots and realize what he was referring to.

"Are you talking about moving her into her own room?" At the beginning of the week, Erin had suggested that he might be able to get more sleep if he moved Marlie's crib into the guest room next to his. It was her tactful way of telling him that he was beginning to look like one of the walking undead.

"That can only be a good thing," Calista assured him. "This way, you don't lie in bed, listening to every breath she takes and Marlie gets used to having her own space."

Jake still looked concerned and somewhat unconvinced. Calista smiled, shaking her head. Jake was obviously one of the good ones.

"She's right in the room next to you, Jake," she reminded him. "It's not like you sent her off to live on the East Coast."

No, but that was what Maggie's parents wanted him to do. Send his daughter off with them and they had a home that was way across the country.

Get a grip, he sternly ordered himself.

Calista was right. He *was* being too overprotective. He never used to be like that, he thought. But after what happened to Maggie, he'd had gone through a crisis of conscience. Still, he recognized being so overprotective had to be grating on the nerves.

"You probably think I'm an idiot," he told Calista. His words were accompanied by a defensive shrug.

"I think," she began slowly, contradicting him, "that you are a kind, patient, loving man who's trying to learn all the different facets of being a father all at once. You're demanding too much of yourself. This kind of thing doesn't happen overnight."

He was grateful to her. As usual, she'd made him feel better. "You've got a way of putting a good spin on everything."

"I have a way of seeing more than you do," she amended.

Despite his preoccupation, he'd begun to notice something. A pattern was emerging. "You know you have a habit of deflecting compliments?"

She drew herself up a little, unconsciously growing defensive. "No, I don't."

His eyes held hers as his mouth curved. "You're beautiful."

Where had that come from? She'd never thought of herself in that light. "No, I'm not."

It had been a test. Never mind that he was being truthful and actually meant what he'd just said about her looks. She'd reacted exactly the way he'd expected her to.

"See?" he said. "You're deflecting."

"And you're delusional—" She paused as things fell together for her. "Unless you just made that up to prove a point."

"I was trying to prove a point," he allowed. "But I also meant what I just said." He repeated it in case there was any question as to what he was referring to. "Aside from being that godsend I mentioned earlier, you *are* beautiful."

His voice had dropped down several decibels and she could have sworn that he was all but caressing her with his voice as well as his eyes. She could feel excitement rippling through her.

Anticipation was rising up on tiptoes.

"Just shows that you really are exhausted and desperately need to get some sleep," she told him just a bit too flippantly. Despite what she'd just said, she was really hoping he wouldn't agree and just go to sleep on her. She wanted to talk a bit longer, linger her a bit longer.

"Not that exhausted. And I'll say the same thing in

the morning. Feel the same way in the morning," Jake added softly. Very gently, he cupped her cheek, turning her head until she had no choice but to look up into his eyes. "I don't know what I'd do without you, Calista," he told her with feeling.

"You have Erin," she whispered.

Even as she spoke, she could feel her insides begin to tremble, set in motion by the wave of intense yearning that had washed over her. She was trying to rein in her emotions, but even as she struggled, she knew it was a losing battle. She wanted him too much. Wanted to feel him wanting her too much.

"Erin's wonderful and I'm grateful to her for opening up her home to Marlie and me, but Erin has no more experience with babies than I do," he pointed out patiently, wanting her to accept her due. It was important to him. "You're the one with all the answers."

No, I'm not. I haven't got a single answer as to what to do with these feelings I have for you.

Out loud, Calista did what he'd come to expect. She denied his assertion. "No, I'm not."

"You're doing it again," he told her, moving in just a tad closer to her on the sofa. Moving in until their shadows merged into one. "You're deflecting."

"Because you're giving me too much credit," she countered.

He disagreed. "I'm just telling you the truth." He smiled into her eyes. "You know, 'the truth shall set you free,' that kind of thing."

She could feel his smile go straight into her soul. The rest of her held its breath.

Waiting.

Hoping.

"Oh, I don't know," she heard herself saying. "Sometimes it just traps you instead. Better not to say anything and just play it by ear, take one step at a time." *Like I am with you,* she added silently.

Jake lightly brushed his fingertips along her cheek, hopelessly arousing her. And then he surprised her by saying, "I want to kiss you, Calista."

Did he expect her to say no? To tell him that he couldn't? Couldn't he see how she felt?

"Go ahead," she whispered, almost afraid to believe what was happening. What she was feeling. She couldn't tear her eyes away from his mouth as he spoke. She could all but feel his lips on hers. "No one's going to stop you."

He was having a very difficult time being noble.

Desires larger than his initial intentions to be good kept rising up and demanding their due.

"You should be," he managed to tell her, his breath warm on her face, on her neck.

Calista felt her stomach muscles tightening like a clenched fist, all but completely terminating her ability to breathe.

"Why?" she wanted to know.

Couldn't Jake tell that she was barely holding on? That all she wanted was to have him kiss her? Kiss her over and over again until she melted? To have him make love with her until there was nothing but steam left in her wake? Contented steam.

"Because I'm no good for you," he told her, agony twisting his very gut. He felt torn in half. There was no denying that he wanted her, but there was also no denying that what he'd just said to her was true. He really felt he wasn't any good for her.

"That's up to me to decide," she told him hoarsely, her emotions, her need to be with him, all but choking her.

There was only one way to make her understand. He had to tell her. "I was in love with Maggie," he confessed. "And now she's dead," he pronounced heavily.

Did he really believe there was some kind of eerie connection? The man was too intelligent to think that way. But then, sometimes the heart took over when the mind couldn't.

Sympathy for what he was going through filled her. "The two are not mutually exclusive," she told him quietly.

He looked at her, unconvinced despite the fact that he really wanted to be persuaded. "Are you so sure?"

He was desperately trying to talk himself out of something they both wanted, she thought. Her determination to bring him over to her side mushroomed. She wasn't about to allow his guilt to dictate what happened here tonight. Not after he'd come so far.

Not when she was so close.

"Never more sure of anything in my life," she whispered, her voice brimming with untapped desire.

If he was still convinced that he was in the right and thus determined to continue his protest, Jake never got the opportunity.

Afraid he was going to withdraw at the last moment, Calista went into action. She did the only thing she could. She sealed her mouth to his and with that one solitary deed, irrevocably sealed both their fates as well.

The moment the kiss became a reality, it instantly ignited a fire within Jake. A fire that had existed, not quite dormant, just beneath the surface all this time. A fire that now exploded, threatening to consume both of them whole.

Jake struggled not to contain the desire erupting within him, which was all but impossible, but to keep it from getting the upper hand. He didn't want Calista to think he was some kind of a sex-starved creature, out to satisfy his cravings no matter what.

What was of foremost importance to him was that what happened between them be of paramount pleasure for her. That she look back at tonight not with confusion or dread, but with at least a small amount of genuine affection. More than anything else, he wanted her to enjoy this.

That he was going to enjoy it went without saying. Just holding her, kissing her, aroused such infinite pleasure within him that he was surprised it didn't break him apart into tiny, shiny little pieces.

"You're sure?" he asked when he finally managed to force himself to draw back for a second. The last thing he wanted was to reward everything she'd done for him by overwhelming her, by stealing away her right to change her mind at the last possible second.

What did it take to convince this man that he wasn't forcing himself on her? Calista wondered. That if anything, she was the one doing the forcing?

"I promise I'll have a notary public witness me sign an affidavit to that effect tomorrow if it'll make you feel better." Her eyes held his as she urged, "Just make love with me tonight."

The last thin strand of restraint keeping him away from what he wanted with every fiber of his being snapped, leaving the path utterly clear for him.

A rush of emotions took possession of him as Jake began kissing her over and over again. Kissing her face, her hair, her throat. Kissing the tempting expanse of skin along the shoulders that suddenly became exposed to him when he tugged away the royal blue peasant blouse she had on.

And as his lips moved along her body, feeding rather than quenching his desire, he could feel her hands on him. Feel her struggling to free him of the confinement created by his clothing.

Struggling to be able to touch his body free of false barriers.

Deep shivers flashed and shimmied along his spine as he felt Calista's fingers splaying out, branding his flesh as they passed over his body, seemingly taking inventory and memorizing everything.

And each and every pass of her hands just made his

body temperature rise even further until he was certain that he was going to burn to a crisp.

As much as she wanted to draw this out, to savor every second as she committed every ridge, every dip along his body to tactile memory, that was equally as much as she wanted to rush, to do it all quickly at least this once, before something happened to make it stop, so that she would have it forever.

And if possible, she wanted to do it all again, from the beginning.

But at least this one time.

Because he made her feel the way no one ever had before—just as she had known, deep down in the bottom of her soul, that he would.

Calista felt as if her entire body was singing as he undressed her, recklessly tossing her clothing aside even as she tugged away material from his body, matching him item for item, stroke for stroke.

Was he as excited as she was? she wondered. Was he as eager? She could feel his heart pounding beneath her palm and it sent shockwaves through her. Her own heart was racing and she had to remind herself to breathe.

Somehow, without her knowing just how, they had managed to go from the sofa to the floor, their bodies as tangled with one another as their clothes were. The tempo continued to increase, fueled by a sense of urgency. Did he feel it, too? Or was he just following her lead? Questions filled her head and then fled.

Everything left but this overwhelming need that demanded to be fed.

A need that only he could satisfy.

Their tempo went from fast to fever pitch as she felt his hands caressing her. Possessing her. She almost cried out in wonder as she felt climax flower into climax just from the feel of him, from the way his hands and his lips made love to her.

She did her best to return the favor, to fan the flames she could see he felt, fan them as urgently as he'd fanned hers.

Another climax rocked her and she arched her body into his, silently urging him to take her, silently conveying that she couldn't hold back another moment. She *needed* to be one with him.

A moan escaped her lips as Jake wove his fingers through hers and then drove himself into her, first slowly, then faster and faster.

The journey to the top of the summit was swift, urgent and entirely mind-numbing. She thought she might have cried out, but she wasn't sure.

For a good three minutes if not more, Calista was certain that her heart would never get back to any kind of a normal rhythm, never get back to a normal beat. She recalled thinking that a hummingbird's wings went at a slower pace.

The heat created by the all-but-out-of-body experience finally began to retreat, wave by wave, leaving her colder and colder until it finally vanished and reality marched into her life.

She was almost afraid to open her eyes and look at Jake. Afraid of what she might see.

Would he just withdraw from her? Act as if this hadn't happened? She'd heard that some men did things like that, that the more they seemed to be affected by what happened during the act of lovemaking, that was how much they were into denying that it ever did.

She wasn't sure what to expect.

Taking a fortifying breath and offering up a small, silent prayer, Calista finally opened her eyes.

And found that Jake had propped himself up on his elbow. Instead of staring off into space, he was looking directly down into her face. His expression was unreadable.

What did that mean? Was it a good sign? Or a bad one?

Was he disappointed?

Oh please, God, don't let him be disappointed. I know I couldn't have been the best woman he's ever had, but at least don't let me be a major disappointment in his eyes.

When he finally spoke, his words came slowly, as if they were each being carefully measured out before they were allowed to emerge.

"That was really fast." Jake took a breath. And then he said the two words that slashed at her heart. The two words, more than any other two words, that she *did not* want to hear. "I'm sorry."

Chapter Thirteen

The two ugly words echoed in her head, even as they seemed to burn into her flesh.

Until this moment, she would have said that everything that had transpired prior to now, every step that she had taken, every situation she had been in, had all been pointing to this, to making love with him.

Her body was still bathed in the afterglow, still tingling from the shared ecstasy. But now Jake, with those two terrible words he had just uttered, had stolen her joy, ripped it right out from under her.

Afraid she was going to cry, Calista bolted upright. Willing the tears that were burning her eyes into temporary retreat, she immediately began to gather her clothes to her.

All she wanted was to get away from him so that he couldn't see her break down.

Confused by the sudden shift in her behavior, Jake caught her wrist just as she was about to stand up. What had just happened here? Why was she being so abrupt when he was trying to apologize?

"Where are you going?" he wanted to know.

She kept her face averted, struggling to keep her voice even. "Home."

He felt the urgency in her body. "Why?" he asked, then realized that sounded unduly harsh. He hadn't meant for it to come out like that. She had a perfect right to go home, but he couldn't help wondering if he'd offended her somehow. "I mean, why now?"

What was he doing, playing games now? Oh, the hell with it. If she cried, she cried. Turning her head, Calista glared at him. "Well, you just said you were sorry you made love with me, so I thought I'd spare you the sight of having to look at me any longer."

He stared at her, dumbfounded and, just for a moment, speechless. "Sorry that I— That we— No," he finally declared with feeling despite his very real confusion that prevented him from forming a coherent sentence. "No, I didn't," he insisted. "Where did you even *get* an idea like that?"

Why was he playing dumb? "Well, you just said you're sorry."

And he was. Wholeheartedly. "Yes," he agreed, waiting for her to continue.

Frustrated, she blew out a breath. "Okay, I'm

officially confused. If you're not saying you're sorry we just made love, then what *are* you saying you're sorry about?"

"That we made love so fast." He'd thought that was clear. Obviously not.

As Calista slowly began to relax, he drew her back against his shoulder and lay down again. One of the sofa's pillows had fallen on the floor during the course of their lovemaking and he tucked it beneath his head now, creating a small island of comfort for them.

"Our first time should have been a lot slower," he told her.

"Our first time," she repeated. Calista turned her head to look up at him. "As in there's going to be another time?"

He laughed softly, amused by her innocence. "After that kind of 'first time,' you better believe there's going to be another time." And then he amended his statement, just in case. "Unless you don't want there to be."

She nestled into him. The world was suddenly rosy again. The smile on her lips crept into her eyes as she looked up at him. She fervently wished she could freeze time right at this moment.

"I never said that."

"Good." He slowly drew his fingers along her cheek, loving the feel of her. "Because I was thinking, seeing as how there's a lull and everything, that maybe the second time could start now."

A giddy laugh hitched in her throat, spreading out

to all parts of her as she turned her body into his. "Anytime you're ready."

"Perfect, because I'm ready now," he told her.

But just as he drew her even closer to him, a sliver of common sense pierced its way through the flood of desire, causing him to stop and glance toward the front door. There was no reason in the world to think that Erin and Corey would be back before Sunday evening—most likely late Sunday evening—but he had always preferred erring on the side of safety.

If his sister and her husband walked in on him at an inopportune moment, other than some embarrassment all around, it was no big deal. But he didn't want either of them catching Calista in this sort of compromising position.

"Why don't we see what this feels like on a bed?" he suggested.

Calista grinned, catching the corner of her bottom lip between her teeth. She had no idea how much that small, inconsequential action tempted him—at least, not until she saw desire flare in his eyes.

"I had no idea you had this kinky side to you," she teased.

"Stick around," he promised. "You might be surprised."

What surprised her most of all was that he had just asked her to stick around. The phrase had long-term implications.

As they hurried up the stairs, each holding their

clothes tightly against them in their arms, every part of her was smiling. Broadly.

As it turned out, Calista never did manage to go home that weekend. Because she still had her overnight case with a couple of changes of clothing in her trunk from the last trip she'd taken a few months ago, she didn't need to make a stop at her house for fresh laundry.

But because she knew her family would worry if she didn't report in, she did call. As she dialed, Calista crossed her fingers, hoping that she'd find herself talking to the answering machine instead of one of her siblings. Answering machines, at least, didn't ask questions.

Luck turned out to be with her and no one picked up the phone when she called home. That left her free to say that she was "putting in extra hours at work" and that she would see them when she was finished, "whenever that turns out to be."

"Is that what you call it now?" Jake asked her, amused, when she hung up. He'd been walking by in the hallway to get yet another change of clothes for Marlie who'd spat up when he'd heard Calista on the phone in his bedroom. When she raised a quizzical eyebrow in response, he elaborated. "Extra hours at work?"

An impish smile played on her lips. "Well, technically, you did hire me to babysit Marlie," she reminded him. Her smile widened as she spoke.

She'd found herself smiling this entire weekend,

happy beyond words. The moment Marlie was down for the night, she would discover paradise all over again in Jake's arms. Calista couldn't remember *ever* being quite this happy and she was by nature a happy person. But being with Jake—despite his more serious moods at times—took her beyond the realm of happy to a place she had never known existed until now.

Despite the fact that everything was still exceedingly fresh and new between them, in her heart Calista was certain that she had found the person she was meant to be with forever.

The trick, she knew, was going to be in making Jake realize it as well. She was prepared to wait for that no matter how long it took. Happiness of this caliber was worth waiting for—and worth fighting for, if it came down to that.

"You know—"

Whatever he was going to say to her was temporarily placed on hold as a buzzing noise suddenly started coming from the cell phone he'd left on his bureau. Rather than have it ring, he'd left it on vibrate. And it did. As the urgent sound repeated, the vibrations propelled the phone along the surface of the bureau, moving it closer and closer to the edge like a suicidal lemming.

Jake caught it just before it went over the side, sparing it landing unceremoniously on the rug. Without bothering to look at the caller's ID—he assumed it had to be his sister calling—Jake opened the phone as he crossed over to the bed, pressed the virtual button accepting the call and said, "Hello?"

The deep voice on the other end of the line told him this wasn't his sister even before the man asked, "Is this Jake Castro?"

Calista saw tension telegraph throughout Jake's body just as he sat down beside her. It was as if every fiber of his being had gone on alert.

"Yes, this is Jake."

Calista mouthed "Who is it?" but he just shrugged in response, indicating that he had no idea who was on the other end of the line.

Ignorance faded away in the next moment as the voice on the other end demanded, "Did you think we'd give up just because you took off with her and dropped out of sight?"

Jake could feel his stomach muscles tighten so hard that for a minute it robbed him of his breath. He held the cell phone with both hands even though he was tempted just to throw it against the wall and watch it smash into impotent little pieces.

Observing him, Calista didn't have to ask again who he was talking to, or rather who he was listening to. His body language told her. One of Maggie's parents had to be on the other end of the line.

Concerned, she moved closer to him. She put her hand on his knee, silently trying to convey her support. Wishing that she could *do* something for him. But for now, all she could do was to be here.

"No," Jake finally snapped into the phone. "I came here because my family's here. I thought being around family would be good for my daughter."

"What would be good for our granddaughter," Maggie's father retorted with authority, deliberately eliminating the baby's connection to the man he was talking to and emphasizing the baby's connection to him, "is to be with people who know what they're doing. That means not being around a group of fumbling, barely post-adolescence people who haven't a clue about what it actually takes to raise a child."

Jake didn't bother with denials, with retorting that he had experienced help, *very* experienced help, in Calista, who also happened to be the mayor's cousin. Saying so would only be wasting his breath because Maggie's father wasn't the type of man to listen to anything but the sound of his own voice.

But Jake wanted the man to know that he didn't appreciate being spied on. How else could O'Shea have found out where he and Marlie were unless the man had hired a professional snoop to spy on him and his family and friends?

Just thinking about it made Jake angry.

"How much are you paying that private investigator of yours to spy on us?" he asked contemptuously.

"Doesn't matter," O'Shea dismissed. "It's all worth it now that he's located you." And then he laughed to himself, obviously pleased that he had rattled his granddaughter's father. "What's the point of having money if you can't use it to help you?" he asked flippantly. "If you're as smart as Maggie claimed you were, you'll give up now. I've got a lot more money than you do and it's for damn sure we're going to get better legal representation than you can afford.

"Besides," O'Shea continued, giving Jake a summation of what lay ahead if he did choose to fight for custody of the little girl, "Gloria and I have the established lifestyle as well as the friends and the connections. Face it, we've got you beat, boy. Who do you think the judge is going to go with? Well-off, stable grandparents or a father who doesn't even have his own place?"

Jake struggled not to let his temper explode. "I'm staying with my sister and her husband."

"Exactly. No place of your own. You sublet your apartment. The lease will be up on that soon. That leave of absence you're on will dry up and you'll just be another statistic. You want that kind of life for Marlie?"

Calista caught him by the wrist, trying to get his attention. She'd pieced things together from his side of the conversation and the few loud words she'd overheard coming from Harry O'Shea.

"What?" Jake demanded sharply, frustrated.

"Ask to meet with them one-on-one, without lawyers," she told him.

He didn't see what good that would do. From everything Maggie had ever told him, O'Shea wasn't a man who could be reasoned with, but he did as she asked. "Can we just get together and see if we can resolve this?"

"It would already be resolved if you'd just admit that we can give Marlie a lot more than you can." There was a pause for a moment, and then O'Shea said, "Okay, we're willing to see you. Maybe we can come to some kind of an arrangement without having to squander any more money on outside parties." His inference was clear. O'Shea meant that *he* was going to have to be the one who ultimately came around.

Suggesting the time and place, both of which were grudgingly acceptable to the older man, Jake hung up. He felt drained as well as cornered. Looking at Calista, he shook his head.

"I should just use the time to grab Marlie and make a run for it. Really disappear this time." Because up until now, that really hadn't been his intention. But the threat he'd heard in O'Shea's voice was real. The man intended to separate him from his daughter. Permanently. He couldn't allow that to happen.

Calista shook her head. Going into hiding with his daughter wasn't a good idea and Jake knew it, she thought. He couldn't spend the rest of his life looking over his shoulder. What kind of a life would that be for him, not to mention for Marlie?

"Your late partner's parents will only track you down," she pointed out.

He didn't know about that. "Maybe not. There're still places in this country where a man could just disappear."

He would know about that better than she would, Calista conceded. But that still didn't change the bottom line: that taking up that kind of life was really no life at all.

"Is that the kind of life you want for Marlie?" she asked him point-blank.

"If it meant that I could keep her in my life, then yes."

"You don't have to resort to such drastic measures to keep her," she reminded him quietly. They'd already discussed this. Had he forgotten? "You said that the key to keeping Marlie is to demonstrate to the presiding judge that you can provide a stable, loving home life for your daughter."

Restless, worried, Jake began to pace around the bedroom. "I know what I said, but O'Shea practically told me he's going to use his money to show that he and his wife are the ones who can offer Marlie a far more stable life than I can." There was anger in his eyes as he spoke. He felt as if the deck was stacked against him. "They're settled, I'm not."

"You're not an unfit parent," she pointed out with feeling. "The courts are always more inclined to leave a child with her biological parent as long as there's no indication of child abuse, neglect or endangerment. And there isn't. You've got a good reputation and look, you've even taken a leave of absence just to devote yourself to learning the ropes on how to be a good parent. You can get character witnesses by the droves to line up and testify on your behalf."

Calista could see that he really wanted to believe what she was saying, wanted to think it was all going to turn out all right, but a deep, underlying fear was holding him back.

She had one more card to play. "And if all else fails, we still have that ace up our sleeve."

He looked at her sharply. Had he missed something? "Which is?"

How could he have forgotten? she wondered. "You can produce a wife to show the court just how serious you are about providing a stable, wholesome atmosphere for your daughter."

"Produce a wife," Jake repeated, then laughed shortly. "Right. Just as soon as I marry one."

Did that mean he remembered their conversation, or was he just making a general wisecrack? Her eyes met his, but she was unable to determine the answer.

"Exactly."

Several weeks had gone by since she'd made that initial offer. At the time, he'd thought she'd said it just to make him feel better. And even if she half meant it when she'd offered, he'd assumed they'd gone passed that.

The parameters of their relationship had certainly changed. They'd become closer and more intimate. Holding her to an offer of a marriage of convenience, for lack of a better term, just wasn't something he felt that, in good conscience, he could do. Especially not when he was convinced that she'd only been joking or flippant when she'd made him the offer. That kind of thing—a marriage of convenience—just wasn't done these days.

But one look at Calista's face told him that she

wasn't kidding. Dumbfounded, he stared at her. "You're actually serious."

Why on earth would he think she'd be kidding about something that had such consequences for him? Something that could ultimately involve the fate of his daughter? "Yes, of course I am."

For one moment, Jake was sorely tempted. Marrying Calista would help solve his immediate problem and who knew? The play-acting involved could eventually lead to other things....

But then he shook his head. This wasn't right. "I can't ask you to do that for me."

"You're not," she insisted. "I'm offering. As a last resort, if you will, and nothing in your present life will have to change," she promised. "You can still go on with your life the way it was or whatever way you'd like it to be," she amended because she hadn't seen him with anyone else.

Privately she knew it would be hard turning a blind eye to her "husband" seeing other women, but she wasn't about to start weaving fairy tales for herself. She was doing a pragmatic thing to save his child. She had no right to expect him to remain faithful to her if all they were doing was getting married in name only.

For now, Jake shut his mouth. He'd come to learn that arguing with Calista was like trying to mine gold standing in quicksand. It couldn't be done. So for the time being, he surrendered, agreeing that if all else failed, he would take out a license, seek out a justice of the peace and the two of them would get married.

In the meantime, he began to make plans as to what he was going to say once he came face-to-face with Marlie's grandparents.

Chapter Fourteen

Initially, Maggie's parents had requested that Jake meet with them in their hotel room, but that, he felt, gave the older couple a home-court advantage. He suggested something more neutral where neither of them had an advantage over the other.

His years on the New Orleans police force had taught him to consider all contingencies and made him exceedingly suspicious. When Calista made the suggestion that they get together in a public park, where the open space would prevent him from being caught off guard by any additional parties who might be waiting—or hiding—out of sight, he immediately agreed.

When he smiled his approval and said, "I've got you thinking like a cop now," just before he called the O'Sheas back, she knew he meant it as high praise. A warm feeling spread all through her as she listened to him make the final arrangements on the phone.

They both had a penchant for being early. Arriving at the park for what Jake considered the most important meeting of his life was no different. He, Calista and the baby were there a good twenty minutes ahead of the agreed-upon time. And ten minutes ahead of Harry O'Shea and his wife, Gloria.

When the latter couple arrived, O'Shea immediately scowled when he saw Calista sitting on the bench beside Jake.

"You said no lawyers," he accused Jake, his florid face pulled into a deep scowl even as it turned red.

Jake rose to his feet pugnaciously. "And I didn't bring one," he bit off, struggling to be civil.

"Oh no? Then who's she?" O'Shea contemptuously jerked a thumb at Calista.

"She's my—"

Whether Jake was about to say "backup" or "friend," Calista didn't know, but her gut instincts told her that whatever term he was going to apply to her wasn't going to get the proper reaction needed in this situation. So she beat him to the punch and interjected, "Fiancée," before Jake could answer.

"Fiancée?" Mrs. O'Shea repeated, clearly surprised. She exchanged looks with her husband; hers was flustered and distressed. They both knew what producing a fiancée before the presiding judge would mean. A shift of weight to Jake's case.

"What are you trying to pull?" O'Shea demanded hotly, still on his feet.

"Please, sit," Calista urged the older couple. "We're not trying to pull anything," she assured them, her tone low, soothing, as if she were trying to lull a cranky, crying child to stop fussing. "Actually, this all came about a few weeks ago, when Jake came home with his daughter. Our families both have their roots here. We've known each other for most of our lives."

It was a lie and she was surprised at just how smoothly, how easily it seemed to come to her tongue. She and Jake had never interacted directly, had never taken note of one another before, but their families *did* live here. And if she was embellishing on the rest to help Jake keep his little girl, she felt she could be forgiven.

After a beat, first Mrs. O'Shea, and then, reluctantly, her husband, sat down on the bench opposite them.

Relieved, Calista smiled to herself as she continued with her narrative for O'Shea's benefit.

"When Jake came home with Marlie, the timing just seemed right somehow." She focused her efforts on Mrs. O'Shea who she sensed was the more approachable of the two. "I'm from a large family and I can't remember a time when I wasn't pitching in to help raise my younger siblings." She cut a few corners in her narrative, saying, "Jake asked for my help and I was happy to lend him a hand. I'd done a lot of growing up since I saw him last and Jake had mellowed out a bit." She looked down pointedly at Marlie. The little girl, strapped into her carryall, was on the bench between her and Jake. "Due, in no small part, to becoming the father of a newborn."

"Very touching," O'Shea commented sarcastically, clearly not moved. "But you forgot to bring along some guys to play the violin while you told your story."

"Harry," his wife cried, embarrassed. O'Shea only waved her into silence.

"Can't you see they're playing you, Gloria?" he demanded in disgust. "I wasn't born yesterday or the day before," he informed the younger couple angrily. "You're just marrying her because you think the judge will let you keep Marlie if you can show her how 'stable' you are because you're 'married,'" O'Shea concluded in a mocking, singsong voice.

Calista exchanged looks with Jake. Had he caught that? Or had she misheard that slip in the older man's rant?

She hadn't misheard. Jake had picked up on it, too. The next moment she heard Jake suspiciously asking O'Shea, "How do you know the judge is a her?"

Caught, O'Shea attempted to bluster his way out of the blunder. He shrugged dismissively. "Or him. Gotta be one or the other, right?"

"Right," Calista agreed. "But most people assume the judge is a male." *Especially if they come across as opinionated chauvinists, like you.*

"But you didn't. You wouldn't be trying to tamper with the judicial process, now would you, Mr. O'Shea?" Jake asked him. The supposedly innocent question was mingled with just enough sarcasm to let the older couple know that that was *exactly* what he thought they were doing. "Because if that's true, you're going to wind up losing all rights to Marlie, including visitation. The courts frown on jury tampering. Think how much more displeased they'll be over your trying to bribe a judge," he suggested.

"Harry didn't bribe a judge," his wife cried. Then, feeling slightly uncertain, she slanted a quick look at her husband. "You didn't, did you, Harry?"

"Of course not!" the man blustered.

Jake recalled that Maggie had once told him her father believed that the best defense was a strong offense and that was exactly what was going on here, he thought. O'Shea, a stocky bull of a man who'd once been an amateur boxer in his early twenties, drew himself up to his full formidable size.

Glaring at Jake, he demanded, "Are you threatening me, boy?"

"No one's threatening anybody," Calista interjected in her calm, sensible voice. "All we're doing here is just reviewing the facts."

She was hoping to defuse the situation before it became too heated. She glanced toward O'Shea's wife, hoping to arouse a reluctant ally. After all, if her husband did something that would get him barred from seeing his grandchild, she would find herself included in that ruling.

After a beat, the woman placed a restraining, imploring hand on her husband's arm. "Harry, maybe we should hear them out. After all, he was Margaret's partner."

"Some partner," the man spat with disdain. He glared at the man who wanted to take his granddaughter away. "Where were you the day my daughter was shot by that slimy scumbag lowlife, huh?" he demanded, shouting now. "Where *were* you?"

Didn't they know? Or had they just forgotten? "Maggie asked to switch partners," Calista informed the late officer's parents.

Jake seemed not to hear her. Instead, he answered the underlying question within O'Shea's angry demand. "Not a day goes by that I don't regret what happened to Maggie. That I don't wish it had been me instead of her."

O'Shea glared at him. Calista saw tears shining in the man's eyes. "That makes two of us," O'Shea bit off angrily.

"Sir, your daughter requested and got a new partner when she went back to active duty," Calista pointed out again when it became obvious to her that her initial words hadn't registered with O'Shea. She knew that because he felt riddled with guilt about Maggie's death, Jake wasn't about to defend himself. It was up to her to make the O'Sheas understand, she thought. "There was no way Jake could have been there to protect your daughter without breaking protocol."

O'Shea scowled as he took in the information. She'd been right, Calista thought, he hadn't heard her and no one had told him about Maggie switching partners.

"Why did she ask for another partner?" O'Shea asked suspiciously, then instantly supplied his own partial explanation. "What did you do to her?"

Calista looked at Jake, her expression telling him that if he didn't say something, she would. Resigned, Jake told them what Maggie obviously hadn't. "I asked her to marry me."

"You—you what?" Mrs. O'Shea asked, dumbfounded. She looked both surprised and disappointed.

He was a private person by nature and as such, didn't like sharing bits of himself like this, especially not on demand to explain himself to a man who was obviously an emotional bully. But he sensed that Calista knew what she was doing when she spilled these particular beans. She was trying to prevent this from having to go to court, from having Marlie become a human rope in what threatened to be an emotional tug-of-war.

"I asked her to marry me," he finally repeated, his voice low, emotionless even as the memory generated a tidal wave of feelings within him. "I told her that Marlie deserved two parents and that I wanted to be able to take care of both of them. Maggie said that wasn't the deal we'd made and that if I couldn't honor it, if I was going to go back on my word, I left her no choice but to request a new partner."

He drew in a long, shaky, angry breath, trying to center himself.

Under control, he concluded, "*That's* why I wasn't there the day she was shot."

Calista's heart ached for him. She sensed that

admitting to this, to Maggie's rejection of his proposal and the consequences that inadvertently ensued because of that rejection, cost him a great deal.

For a moment, O'Shea seemed to mull over this new piece of information, but then a second wave of anger visibly washed over him. His eyes narrowed as they focused on Calista with contempt.

"Recovered pretty fast from my daughter's rejection, didn't you?" Before Jake could ask what he was talking about, O'Shea nodded toward Calista. "Asking this one to marry you when my daughter's body is hardly cold," he said contemptuously. "Or is this all a game to you?"

"Harry, please," Mrs. O'Shea half chided, half pleaded with her husband for him to be more civil. When he looked at her accusingly, she addressed her words to all three of them. "When I first found out what Maggie wanted to do—to have a baby in such a practical, sterile fashion—I was dead set against it. It just didn't seem right to me. She tried to win me over to her side, telling me what a good man you were, Jake," she said, looking at him. "And that there wasn't anyone she would have wanted to father her child more than you." Her voice caught, but she pushed forward. Tears began to fall from her eyes as she remembered one of the last conversations she'd had with her daughter. "She told me that Jake had all the qualities she wanted her baby to have. I still told her not to go through with it, to wait until she found someone she wanted to marry, to have a family with." She wiped away a tear. "But she went ahead anyway.

And thank God she did, because now, at least I still have a part of her," she concluded with a sob.

O'Shea blew out a long breath and made an unintelligible disparaging noise. "If that's true, if she found him so 'wonderful,' why didn't she want to marry him?" he challenged his wife.

"Because she didn't want to get married," his wife admitted heavily. "To anyone." Heartsick, Mrs. O'Shea wiped her wet cheeks with the back of her hand. She looked over toward the baby, then, rising, she crossed to Jake. "May I—may I hold her, please?" she asked, her voice cracking slightly.

Nodding, Jake surrendered his daughter to her grandmother. Rather than cross back to her husband with the child, Gloria O'Shea sank down on the bench beside Jake.

To Calista the silent deed spoke volumes.

Angry over what he'd just heard, angry that his beloved only little girl had been so stubbornly independent, so different from what his own initial projections of what he had wanted her to be, for a few minutes, O'Shea was at a loss for coherent words.

He struggled to collect himself. "Yeah, well, the fact remains that we still can provide the better, more stable life for Marlie."

"No disrespect intended, sir," Calista began, "but your granddaughter needs parents who can keep up with her. She deserves that," she added pointedly.

"What she deserves is a stable life," O'Shea snapped

back. "Not some wet-behind-the-ears woman who's barely out of elementary school herself."

"She'll have that stable life," Jake informed him. "And Calista's a lot older, not to mention wiser, than she looks," he informed Maggie's father coldly, coming to Calista's defense. O'Shea had no right to just dismiss her like that. "There isn't anything I wouldn't do for my daughter, Mr. O'Shea. There aren't any lengths I wouldn't go to to ensure she has everything she needs and deserves."

"Including marrying someone you don't love just to create the illusion of a family?" O'Shea challenged. It was obvious that he still didn't believe him.

Calista began to say something, but Jake held his hand up, signaling he wanted her to hold her peace as he answered.

"Including that," he readily agreed. His next words took everyone by surprise, most of all Calista. "Fortunately, that won't be the case here."

He was turning her down, Calista thought. She felt frustration setting in. He was making a mistake and there wasn't anything she could do to prevent it.

Jake looked toward her for a moment, then said to O'Shea, "Because I've come to realize that I do love Calista."

Had she not suddenly discovered she was frozen in place, Calista was fairly positive that her mouth would have dropped open, with her chin hitting the ground somewhere beside her feet.

It took her a second to realize that Jake was still talking.

"She's shown herself to be in every way a kind, loving, caring woman who loves Marlie and would gladly place Marlie's well-being above her own. Maggie and I had a great many things in common and we shared most of the same experiences on the job together. But what Calista and I share is far broader than that. Maggie gave birth to Marlie, but she couldn't wait to get back to the job. *That* was where her heart was. She was a law enforcement agent first, a mother second. That was what we argued about before she went back to work early. And that was really why she asked for another partner. Because seeing me reminded her that she didn't want to be a mother above all else. That was just one part of her.

"And there's nothing wrong with that," he went on to state. "But it did split us up. I don't feel the same way Maggie did. I'm willing to give up being a cop for Marlie. For all intents and purposes," he told them, "I already have. And I'd do it again. Don't take my daughter from me. I need her and she needs me."

O'Shea opened his mouth twice, but both times he shut it again, as if unsure of what he should say first. Undecided, he looked at his wife for a long moment, as if communicating with her on some different level, the one achieved by a couple who had been together for decades and basically knew each other's thoughts.

"If we drop the suit," O'Shea began after a couple of

false starts, "and let you keep custody of Marlie, when will we be able to see her?"

There was no hesitation on Jake's part. This was never about exclusive control, only in keeping his death-bed promise to Maggie.

"You're her grandparents," Jake said to the couple. "You're part of her life. You can visit her as often as you like."

"She'll grow up a lot happier knowing she's so well loved and not just some ultimate prize in a surreal tug-of-war contest," Calista told the older couple, adding her two cents.

O'Shea was still hedging and it was impossible to see if he'd been won over or if he was just baiting them for some perverse reason.

"And *if* we drop the suit," the man posed, putting a great deal of emphasis on the single two-letter word, "are you two still going to get married?" He looked from one to the other, waiting for a reply, an odd sort of look in his eyes.

He was setting them up with a trick question, Calista thought. Her gut told her that the man wanted to hear an affirmative answer, otherwise he would hold it against Jake, most likely saying that he'd lied just to get them to go along with the arrangement.

But even as she began to say "Yes," the only answer she felt that would work in this scenario, she heard Jake answering his late partner's father for them.

"Yes. Yes, we will." Jake slanted a look in her direction. "Provided that Calista still wants me."

That, her instincts told her, was Jake's way out of this glass prison he'd constructed for himself. He'd remain the man who had all the good impulses and she would be the one who vetoed them. That was how he wanted this to play out.

She didn't fault him. It made things sound more believable. That they'd decided to get married, but if the custody suit was dropped, then the element of extreme urgency was taken out of the equation, leaving them to get married at their own unhurried pace.

All that remained was putting this into words.

So when O'Shea looked at her expectantly, waiting for her to give Jake an answer to the tentative situation he'd outlined—if she still wanted to get married—she had no choice but to say, "Yes, of course I still want to."

Mrs. O'Shea looked almost meek as she spared a glance toward her husband before asking Calista, "Would we be invited to the wedding?"

Calista found herself temporarily at a loss as to how to handle the question. How deeply did she tread into this lie that seemed to be growing by the moment? How much was Jake going to allow or tolerate without finally declaring that enough was enough, that they weren't getting married?

Searching desperately for a way out, for a moment Calista was unaware that Jake had started talking. It wasn't until she realized that he was answering the woman's hesitant question that she began listening more closely.

And then became completely speechless.

"Of course you're invited to the wedding, Mrs. O'Shea."

Marlie began to fuss just then and Calista turned to take her from the older woman. She secretly blessed the child for providing her with an excuse because she needed something to do with her hands until she could recall just how to form words again.

Because right now, her mind was a total blank.

It only became more so as Mrs. O'Shea told her, "That's okay. Let me try to soothe her. It brings back old memories."

Calista had no choice but to back off.

Still too stunned to speak, she stole a look at Jake, wondering what in God's name had prompted the New Orleans police officer to say what he had now that he really didn't have to pretend anymore.

Or did he know something she didn't?

Chapter Fifteen

"So it's settled," Calista said some forty minutes later, wanting, for Jake's sake, to review the points involving Marlie's future that had been negotiated in this park today. "You'll drop the custody suit and allow Marlie to live with us."

She'd almost slipped and said "with Jake," thereby indicating by her slip that she wasn't part of the actual equation, the way the O'Sheas had been led to believe that she was.

It didn't take someone versed in psychology—which she was—to know that the agreement would become null and void for the older couple if they suspected that Jake wasn't about to go through with this proposed marriage. She had no doubt that somewhere down the line— very quickly, actually—he'd come up with a way to convince the couple that even though the marriage had fallen through, he could provide a good, stable home for his daughter.

But for now, they would play this game. "And in exchange, you can come to visit Marlie anytime you like. It'd be easier for you to come here because you're retired and can be more flexible."

"Sounds about right," O'Shea nodded. There were overtones of grousing in his voice, but it appeared that he had made the concession, however grudgingly. Especially because Jake hadn't placed any restrictions on their visitation rights.

"All we ask," Jake added, "is that you give us some warning and call before you come by."

Was that so he could call her to come over and get things ready, enabling them to play their roles? But how was he going to handle the sticky problem about staging a wedding?

O'Shea lumbered over to stand before his wife and look down at his granddaughter, who for the moment had quieted down again. His cottony gray eyebrows drew together in less than an affable line as he threw a glance toward Jake.

"That ain't all you're asking and you know it." He sat down heavily on the other side of his wife. His face softened as he touched Marlie's tiny fisted hand.

Calista noticed that Mrs. O'Shea placed a gentling hand on her husband's wrist, imploring him silently to resolve this matter peacefully for the sake of all concerned.

The latter blew out a frustrated breath, shrugged and said, "But yeah, we'll call ahead and give you a warning so you can hide whatever it is you need to hide from us."

"Mainly it's so I can clean up a little," Calista told him pleasantly. "Things have a tendency to pile up and get a little messy when you're completely focused on taking care of a baby."

O'Shea nodded, appearing to barely hear her. He was looking at Marlie. "I'd better call that lawyer and tell him we won't be needing him." Rising to his feet, signaling an end to the meeting, he looked from Jake to Calista. "But I'm keeping the card just in case."

O'Shea's message was clear. They weren't completely out of the woods yet. The man clearly intended to keep them on their toes when it came to taking care of his granddaughter.

As if he had to, Calista thought.

The two couples walked back together to the parking lot that was behind the park, each attempting to assimilate the agreement that had been reached. For the most part, the matter was resolved, but a residue amount of uncertainty and uneasiness still hung in the air. That was going to take time to work out.

Once Marlie was securely fastened into the backseat, Jake got in on the driver's side, sat down and waited for Calista to secure her own seat belt before starting up the vehicle. With this truce with the O'Sheas finally in place, he able to breathe easier. But there was still a whole list of things to do.

"I'm going to have to call my lieutenant, tell him I'm not coming back," he said as he backed out of the parking spot. "No point in his holding my job for me if I'm going to stay here."

Calista looked at him in surprise. He hadn't mentioned where he planned to live. That he was going to remain in Thunder Canyon thrilled her to no end. "So you're going to stay here permanently?"

"Only makes sense," he confirmed. The look on his face when he glanced at her said he was surprised that she even had to ask. "That means I've got to find a job here." It wasn't a prospect he looked forward to. Ever since he could remember, all he'd ever wanted to be was a cop, but that had to be behind him now. "Maybe I can get a job at the resort."

Calista's jaw dropped in disbelief. "You mean like a regular job-job?" She couldn't begin to picture Jake working there. As what? The bellhop? The desk clerk? It just wasn't him.

"Yes, like a regular job-job." He tried to pretend that the very idea didn't drain his soul.

He was kidding, wasn't he? "And give up police work?"

Jake stared straight ahead as he drove back to his sister's house. He told himself to focus strictly on the victory that had been won today. A victory made that much smoother by the woman who was busy grilling him right now. "Yes."

There wasn't going to be a punch line to this, was

there? He was serious. "But you love being a cop," she protested.

"I've got Marlie to think of."

She knew what he was saying. That police work was dangerous and that Marlie had already lost one parent because of the hazards of law enforcement. He probably figured it would be selfish of him to continue in his line of work.

She saw it differently. "Marlie wouldn't want to see you unhappy because of her. And if Maggie were here, she'd tell you not to give it up, either. She didn't."

That was just his point. "And look where it got her."

If danger was what was holding him back, she doubted if it was much of a factor around here. Law enforcement agents were more likely to die of old age or boredom in Thunder Canyon than of a gunshot wound.

"Did you know that there's an opening on the Thunder Canyon police force?" she asked him. His surprised glance in her direction answered her question for her. "Someone with your background would be a shoo-in for the job. Granted, it wouldn't be as exciting as working in New Orleans, but you'd still be in law enforcement. Why don't you put in your application?"

He smiled to himself as a peacefulness came out of nowhere and descended over him. The pieces were all coming together, a good many of them ushered into place by the woman in the passenger seat.

It occurred to Jake that Calista was looking out for him. As she had been since they'd come together because of Marlie. Calista wasn't nearly as young as he'd first thought. And she definitely had a good head on her shoulders. Besides her many other assets.

"I think I will," he told her.

He sounded happy. Good. Calista settled into her seat as the tension drained out of her. "All things considered, that went rather well back there with the O'Sheas." Better, actually, than she'd expected for a first go-round. And then she remembered. They weren't out of the woods yet. "All except for—" She shifted in her seat to look at him. "What are we going to do about the wedding ceremony they're expecting?"

He shrugged, as if that was so insignificant it didn't even merit a moment's concern. "Invite them, like we said."

Was he hallucinating? How did he think they were going to pull this off? With puppets? "For them to attend a wedding, there has to *be* a wedding," she reminded him patiently.

His expression was completely unfazed as he glanced at her and said, "So?"

"So?" she echoed in disbelief. "So there's not going to *be* a wedding."

"Yes, there is," Jake countered. Easing his foot off the gas as they came to a red light, he slanted a look at her. "Isn't there?"

The man was definitely confusing her. He made it sound as if it was already a done deal.

"Wait," she cried, mentally backing up. "Are you telling me that we're going through with this?"

"You were the one who volunteered, remember?"

he reminded her. Was she backing down now? Had it been strictly to help him hang on to Marlie and nothing more? Had he misread the signals he thought she was giving?

"I know, but that was when it looked as if that was the only way you could get to keep Marlie with you." She glanced over her shoulder toward the rear passenger seat where Jake's daughter was securely strapped into her car seat, lulled to sleep by the rhythm of the moving vehicle.

He needed time to process this. "So you're saying you don't want to marry me?"

I would love *to marry you—because you wanted me, not because you needed an accomplice.* "I'm saying Maggie's parents have backed off, which means that you no longer have to go through with this charade."

He gave her another look, a look she couldn't begin to read, just as the light turned green again.

He'd gone from being afraid that what he was feeling for Calista was only because he was in a tailspin over Maggie's death to knowing that he wasn't on the rebound. What he was feeling for this perky, upbeat, resourceful, intelligent woman had absolutely nothing to do with Maggie or rebounds. And as for having anything to do with Marlie, the connection there was only the relief he felt in knowing that Calista loved the baby.

Damn, but for such a simple life, his had gotten way too complicated, he thought.

"Maybe I want to go through with this," he told her quietly.

"You *want* to go through with this?" she echoed, even as she tried to wrap her head about this. There had to be a joke here somewhere.

Jake took a breath. He'd put it out there. There was no backing off now, not after he'd just proposed in effect. "That's what I said."

She heard the words, but the intent just wasn't sinking in. Not on any level that was actually penetrating her brain.

"You *want* to marry me?"

It was a question, not a statement, so he answered it as such, simply.

"Yes, I want to marry you."

"But why?" she pressed. "There's no need to pretend anymore."

Maybe it would go over better if he continued to act as if there was a need for them to go through this, although he had no idea why she was acting like this. "Maggie's parents are expecting to attend a wedding. They're expecting to see us get married. If we renege on that, they might renege on the rest of it."

Okay, so now it was all making some sense. Why hadn't he admitted to this in the first place? "So you *are* marrying me because you want to keep Marlie."

Okay, he thought, enough bantering and waltzing around. A joke was a joke, but he was dead serious. It was time to take a chance and call a spade a spade and not some fancy, expensive garden tool.

"I'm marrying you because I want to keep *you*." That

didn't come out right, he thought. "I mean— Oh hell, you know what I mean."

Frustrated, he pulled over to the side of the road and turned off the ignition key. He didn't want to have a car accident while he was trying to set the course for the rest of his life—and hopefully hers.

"Don't you know me well enough by now to know that I wouldn't have agreed to some cooked-up, phony marriage-on-paper-only scenario to keep Marlie, much as I love the kid? Nothing good can come out of perpetuating a lie. The truth has an ugly way of surfacing when you least expect it."

She was still confused. "But when I volunteered to marry you so you could keep Marlie, you acted like you thought it was a good idea."

"Seemed like the easier way to go at the time," he confessed. "I knew that arguing with you was as pointless as a pigeon trying to fly against the wind. Best-case scenario, arguing with you would just send me spinning off into circles."

"Okay, that explains earlier," she said slowly, doing her best to untangle the various skeins of this so-called proposal of marriage. "But you just went along with it in front of the O'Sheas."

"I know."

She could only come to one conclusion, a conclusion that put her at risk and left her utterly vulnerable, especially if it turned out to be wrong. But she had to ask him.

"Are you—?" She couldn't bring herself to finish

the question, to ask him if he was really asking her to marry him.

"Yes," Jake finally said as the silence threatened to drag on forever.

She felt as if she'd somehow slipped into an alternate universe without noticing it. "You're actually asking me to marry you?"

"That's usually what the head couple does at a wedding," he agreed. "They get married."

Calista searched his face, waiting for him to begin laughing. He didn't. "Did I miss the part where you did the actual asking?" she finally asked.

"The question—and your answer—were kind of taken for granted when you said you would be willing to marry me," he confessed.

"I was agreeing to a marriage of convenience and that is *not* the same thing as saying I'd marry you after you proposed to me." She could feel her heart accelerating in anticipation as she waited for him to either confirm or deny the proposal he seemed to think he had tendered.

Jake debated starting the car again and revisiting this topic later, with a fresh dose of courage. But he couldn't just start up the car and drive away from this. Not really. It had to be ironed out first.

He never thought he'd love someone else again after Maggie broke his heart, not once but twice. The first time when she turned down his proposal, the second when she died on him. At the end, he'd loved Maggie a great deal.

But he loved Calista differently and quite possibly, in the absolute sense, perhaps even more than he had loved Maggie. Because Calista loved him back.

He looked at Calista for a long moment, struggling to pull his thoughts together, wanting to get this right because in all likelihood, although Calista was a forgiving person, he had just one shot at this. And if it fell apart on him...

He wasn't going to allow that to happen. A woman, he thought, deserved to hear a decent marriage proposal. And Calista deserved everything he could give her and so much more. Because she had given him back his identity, his sense of hope and pulled his world together into a neat little package, allowing him to make sense of things again. Allowing him to feel again.

He owed her a great deal. More than he could ever possibly hope to repay. But he intended to try. If he was lucky, it would only take the rest of his life.

"I love you."

Calista's eyes widened and then crinkled into a pleased smile. "Wow, talk about a disarming opening line," she cried appreciatively.

So far so good. Ever so lightly, he skimmed his fingertips along her cheek. Silently telling her things. And then Jake pushed forward.

"And I want, selfishly maybe, to be able to keep, for as long as I can, all the joy you've brought into my life. I figure I've got a better shot of doing that if we get married and I can legitimately keep you close. So yes, to answer your question from the beginning of this conversation, I am asking you to marry me. Not to keep Marlie in my life, but to keep *you* in my life. Because without you, everything else just falls apart, including me. Marry me, Calista. Marry me and keep my world together."

She struggled to keep a straight face as she asked, "So I'm what, superglue?"

"You're anything you want to be as long as you're mine," he told her.

She took a breath, not wanting to blurt out her answer, or shout it out, either. She didn't need to think about it, but she didn't want him thinking that she was so easily gotten. Didn't want him worrying somewhere down the line that she'd gotten swept up in the moment and agreed to something that she was apt to regret once she came to her senses.

Deep in her heart, she already knew that agreeing to marry him was *never* going to be something she would change her mind about.

She was being much too quiet, Jake thought. That worried him. Deeply. He'd never known her to be quiet. Was that a bad sign, then? Was she ultimately trying to find the words that would let him down easy? She needn't bother. There *were* no such words.

He'd already made up his mind that that was going to be impossible. He wasn't going to let her say no. Now that his heart was made up, he was going to find a way to get her to say yes, even if he had to reinvent himself a dozen times a day until she finally found a version of him she wanted to remain with and that she liked.

"You're not saying anything," he finally said, unable to wait any longer.

And then hope rose as he watched a smile creep into her eyes. "That's because I'm giving it to the count of ten."

"Ten?" The woman certainly believed in maintaining an air of mystery. "Why?"

"So you don't think my answer is just a knee-jerk reaction."

"Oh." He nodded as if that actually made sense. A lifetime of acting as if he understood the way her mind worked was standing in front of him and he couldn't be happier. "What number are you up to?"

"Nine."

One more to go. "I had no idea that you counted that slowly."

"I don't usually." She couldn't hold her grin back a second longer. "Okay, ten," she announced. And then the grin turned into a smile. The most beautiful smile he'd ever seen. To say her smile would have lit up a room would have definitely underdescribed her wattage power. It was the kind of smile that could light up whole cities at a time.

And it was aimed at him.

Jake realized that he'd been holding his breath, waiting. Hoping. Now that he'd made up his mind and had given himself permission to love again, there was nothing he wanted more than to have her agree to marry him. "And your answer is?"

Calista feigned indecision and confusion. "Could I hear the question again, please?"

He played along and framed the question properly. "Calista Clifton, will you marry me?"

Enough of this hard-to-get stuff. "Yes," she cried. "Oh, yes!"

"Good answer," he told her as a wave of sunshine spread throughout his soul.

"Just 'good'?" she asked innocently.

Taking advantage of the fact that Marlie was sleeping in the rear of the car and that he'd stopped the vehicle to have this conversation with Calista in the first place, Jake gave in to the very strong urge that he'd been grappling with.

He pulled Calista into his arms and just before he kissed the woman who'd taken possession of his heart, he said, "I'm better at showing than talking."

And he certainly was.

* * * * *

Look for HIS COUNTRY CINDERELLA
by Karen Rose Smith
the next book in
MONTANA MAVERICKS:
THE TEXANS ARE COMING!
On sale September 2011.

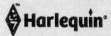

Harlequin®

COMING NEXT MONTH

Available August 30, 2011

SPECIAL EDITION

#2137 HIS COUNTRY CINDERELLA
Karen Rose Smith
Montana Mavericks: The Texans Are Coming!

#2138 HIS TEMPORARY LIVE-IN WIFE
Susan Crosby
Wives for Hire

#2139 IF THE RING FITS
Cindy Kirk
Rx for Love

#2140 CALEB'S BRIDE
Wendy Warren
Home Sweet Honeyford

#2141 HIS MEDICINE WOMAN
Stella Bagwell
Men of the West

#2142 HIS BRIDE BY DESIGN
Teresa Hill

REQUEST YOUR FREE BOOKS!

2 FREE NOVELS PLUS 2 FREE GIFTS!

♦ Harlequin®

SPECIAL EDITION

Life, Love & Family

YES! Please send me 2 FREE Harlequin® Special Edition novels and my 2 FREE gifts (gifts are worth about $10). After receiving them, if I don't wish to receive any more books, I can return the shipping statement marked "cancel." If I don't cancel, I will receive 6 brand-new novels every month and be billed just $4.49 per book in the U.S. or $5.24 per book in Canada. That's a saving of at least 14% off the cover price! It's quite a bargain! Shipping and handling is just 50¢ per book in the U.S. and 75¢ per book in Canada.* I understand that accepting the 2 free books and gifts places me under no obligation to buy anything. I can always return a shipment and cancel at any time. Even if I never buy another book, the two free books and gifts are mine to keep forever.

235/335 HDN FEGF

Name	(PLEASE PRINT)	

Address		Apt. #

City	State/Prov.	Zip/Postal Code

Signature (if under 18, a parent or guardian must sign)

Mail to the **Reader Service:**
IN U.S.A.: P.O. Box 1867, Buffalo, NY 14240-1867
IN CANADA: P.O. Box 609, Fort Erie, Ontario L2A 5X3

Not valid for current subscribers to Harlequin Special Edition books.

Want to try two free books from another line?
Call 1-800-873-8635 or visit www.ReaderService.com.

* Terms and prices subject to change without notice. Prices do not include applicable taxes. Sales tax applicable in N.Y. Canadian residents will be charged applicable taxes. Offer not valid in Quebec. This offer is limited to one order per household. All orders subject to credit approval. Credit or debit balances in a customer's account(s) may be offset by any other outstanding balance owed by or to the customer. Please allow 4 to 6 weeks for delivery. Offer available while quantities last.

Your Privacy—The Reader Service is committed to protecting your privacy. Our Privacy Policy is available online at www.ReaderService.com or upon request from the Reader Service.

We make a portion of our mailing list available to reputable third parties that offer products we believe may interest you. If you prefer that we not exchange your name with third parties, or if you wish to clarify or modify your communication preferences, please visit us at www.ReaderService.com/consumerschoice or write to us at Reader Service Preference Service, P.O. Box 9062, Buffalo, NY 14269. Include your complete name and address.

HSE11B

Rafael de Luca had been in bad situations before. A crowded ballroom could never make him sweat.

These people would never know that he had no memory of any of them.

He surveyed the party with grim tolerance, searching for the source of his unease.

At first his gaze flickered past her, but he yanked his attention back to a woman across the room. Her stare bored holes through him. Unflinching and steady, even when his eyes locked with hers.

Petite, even in heels, she had a creamy olive complexion. A wealth of inky-black curls cascaded over her shoulders and her eyes were equally dark.

She looked at him as if she'd already judged him and found him lacking. He'd never seen her before in his life. Or had he?

He cursed the gaping hole in his memory. He'd been diagnosed with selective amnesia after his accident four months ago. Which seemed like complete and utter bull. No one got amnesia except hysterical women in bad soap operas.

With a smile, he disengaged himself from the group

around him and made his way to the mystery woman.

She wasn't coy. She stared straight at him as he approached, her chin thrust upward in defiance.

"Excuse me, but have we met?" he asked in his smoothest voice.

His gaze moved over the generous swell of her breasts pushed up by the empire waist of her black cocktail dress.

When he glanced back up at her face, he saw fury in her eyes.

"Have we *met?*" Her voice was barely a whisper, but he felt each word like the crack of a whip.

Before he could process her response, she nailed him with a right hook. He stumbled back, holding his nose.

One of his guards stepped between Rafe and the woman, accidentally sending her to one knee. Her hand flew to the folds of her dress.

It was then, as she cupped her belly, that the realization hit him. She was pregnant.

Her eyes flashing, she turned and ran down the marble hallway.

Rafael ran after her. He burst from the hotel lobby, and saw two shoes sparkling in the moonlight, twinkling at him.

He blew out his breath in frustration and then shoved the pair of sparkly, ultrafeminine heels at his head of security.

"Find the woman who wore these shoes."

Will Rafael find his mystery woman?
Find out in Maya Banks's passionate new novel
ENTICED BY HIS FORGOTTEN LOVER
Available September 2011 from Harlequin® Desire®!

Everything Montana Brown *thought* she knew about love and marriage goes awry when her parents split up. Shaken, she heads to Mule Hollow, Texas, to take a chance on an old dream—being a cowgirl…while trying to resist the charms of a too-handsome cowboy. A wife isn't on rancher Luke Holden's wish list. But the Mule Hollow matchmakers are fixin' to lasso Luke and Montana together—with a little faith and love.

Her Rodeo Cowboy
by Debra Clopton

MULE HOLLOW
HOMECOMING